D1099856

The Secret
of the Sleeveen

Cork City Library
WITHDRAWN
FROM STOCK

sleeveen [ˈʃliːviːn] also **sleeveen** (JP, Forth and Bargy), **slíbhín** *n.*, a sly person; a trickster; a smooth-tongued rogue; a toady; a crooked person (LUB, Dublin) < Irish *slíbhín*. 'Look at that sleeveen creeping around the priest—I wonder what he's after now?'; 'Keep away from that sleeveen!' (KG, Kerry).
—Terence Patrick Dolan, 1998. *A dictionary of Hiberno English.: The Irish use of English.* Dublin: Gill & Macmillan.

sleeveen [n. & (more rarely) adj., < Irish *slíbhín* (n.), sly individual]. As thus; term of abuse. **1965** Lee Dunne, *Goodbye to the Hill*: '"You bastard. You sleeveen bastard," he yelled into my face.' **1968** Myles na gCopaleen, *The Best of Myles*: '"You don't hesitate to… denounce me to your even weightier wife as a thief, a fly-by-night, a sleeveen and a baucagh-shool." **1989** Hugh Leonard, *Out after Dark*: '"That fellow's a sleeveen," he said. It was a pejorative word meaning a little mountainy fellow, as treacherous as he was unpredictable.'

"Ah sure 'tis only the Sleeveen"

—Bernard Share, 1997. *Slanguage: a dictionary of slang and colloquial English in Ireland.* Dublin: Gill & Macmillan.

The Secret of the Sleeveen

by Brenda Ennis

Illustrations by
Thomas Ryan

evertype

2013

Published by Evertype, Cnoc Sceichín, Leac an Anfa, Cathair na Mart, Co. Mhaigh Eo, Éire. *www.evertype.com.*

Text © 2013 Brenda Ennis. *www.ancientorderofthesidhe.ie.*

Illustrations © 2013 Thomas Ryan.

This edition © 2013 Michael Everson.

Brenda Ennis has asserted her right under the Copyright, Designs and Patents Act, 1988, to be identified as the author of this work. Thomas Ryan has asserted his right under the Copyright, Designs and Patents Act, 1988, to be identified as the illustrator of this work.

All rights reserved. No part of this publication may be reproduced, stored in a retrieval system, or transmitted, in any form or by any means, electronic, mechanical, photocopying, recording, or otherwise, without the prior permission in writing of the Publisher, or as expressly permitted by law, or under terms agreed with the appropriate reprographics rights organization.

A catalogue record for this book is available from the British Library.

ISBN-10 1-78201-041-6
ISBN-13 978-1-78201-041-8

Typeset in Minion Pro and Ceatharlach by Michael Everson.

Edited by Michael Everson. Advisory editor Mathew Staunton.

Cover: Michael Everson.

Printed by LightningSource.

Contents

ϻy Chanks

- My profound gratitude to the distinctive artist and former president of the Royal Hibernian Academy, Thomas Ryan, a family friend of long-standing, who on hearing of my intention to write this book immediately offered to provide the illustrations. His evocation of the underworld and its citizenry is sometimes playful, sometimes iconic, but always masterly and fascinating.
- To Kelly Fitzgerald PH.D., Lecturer in Folklore and Celtic Civilization, University College Dublin, who acted as consultant on folkloric and traditional material.
- To Seamus Cashman, publisher at Wolfhound Press for 27 years and former chairman of Children's Books Ireland, for his unswerving belief and encouragement in this endeavour.
- To Michael Everson who enjoyed *The Secret of the Sleeveen* sufficiently to publish it.

This book is dedicated to all Irish children, to the children of other Celtic nations and beyond, and especially to Oisin, Tom, Saeve-Louise, and Aaron.

Come with me on this journey outside the realm of everyday existence, connect with the great invisible world, explore our ancient Celtic mythology, question the very foundation of our culture, search for our roots and perhaps enrol with me as a member of the ancient Order of the Sidhe at
www.ancientorderofthesidhe.ie

The Secret
of the Sleeveen

Chapter One

Talk of the *sídhe* is taboo at home

If it wasn't Hallowe'en, it might never have happened. The underworld would have kept its secrets, secrets kept under wraps for thousands and thousands of years. But Hallowe'en it was and Aisling was thrilled to be spending her mid-term break in Eamhain with grandad Aonghus and his sister Meg. Aisling's mum, who insisted on being called Jackie by her only child, was emphatic that this was the last Hallowe'en Aisling would spend with "those weirdos."

"They're the coolest!" Aisling protested. "Why can't you try for dad's sake to be nice to them?"

"Less said, the better," Jackie snapped, adding, "the only reason you're staying in Eamhain is because your aunt Helen's sciatica has flared up again and she can hardly walk, let alone look after you while we go on our Mediterranean cruise."

Aisling couldn't contain her excitement at the prospect of spending Hallowe'en with grandad Aonghus and Meg. She was anxious to quiz her grandad about some thought-provoking artefacts—that's what her dad called them—which she had sneaked a peek at, in his roll-top desk. These included an old family photo-album which she quickly flicked through, some newspaper clippings, and the Ó Dubhghaill family tree chart which traced the family back more than two hundred and sixty years to 1753, when Fionán Mór Ó Dubhghaill married Annie

Murphy. Their ten children, all named, were on the second line of the chart. Little arrows branched outwards and forked downwards and showed all the different generations.

The family almost died out during the 1840s but, thanks to Conán Maol Ó Dubhghaill, Aisling's great-great-grandfather, and Margaret Dillon, the line was carried forward during the Famine years. Hand-written notes beside some of the names recorded unusual events and caught her interest. Abigail (born 1916) died soon after birth. James (born 1935) was drowned, and Róisín (born 1941) was murdered. Wow! Aisling's own name was near the bottom of the chart. She fingered her way back up the line of arrows to her mother's and father's names, Jacqueline Jones and Seán Ó Dubhghaill, and up again from her dad's name to Aonghus Ó Dubhghaill and Bláithín Ní Mhurchú (missing, presumed dead, 1965). Shock! Horror! No one had ever told her that! Bláithín, her grandmother, could still be alive!

She couldn't quiz dad about her discovery. She didn't dare let him know that his "Little Miss Prying Eyes", as he often called her, was poking her nose into his stuff again. She couldn't ask uncle Micheál who lived in the States where he was professor of genealogy at Harvard. He had drawn up the chart and given them a copy of it last summer when they holidayed there. "Eco-friendly green-bin for this chart when we're back home," Jackie, who didn't care whose feelings she trampled on, announced once Micheál was out of earshot.

Aisling folded the chart, opened out the first of the faded newspaper clippings, and read as follows:

> 2 November 1965.
> Search for *sídhe* lore expert called off. Bláithín, wife of Aonghus Ó Dubhghaill, mother of Seán and Micheál, has mysteriously disappeared without trace and is presumed dead. Heavy snow and ice have forced search and rescue volunteers to cancel their search for Bláithín, headmistress of Eamhain National School.

On hearing the key turn in the front door, she quickly popped everything back in the desk and scooted up to her room. That evening, at dinner time, she raised the topic of the *sídhe*.

"Don't let me hear you use that word in this house again," Jackie snapped, "or you'll find yourself grounded for a week." Aisling didn't dare mention the family tree chart, or she would have been grounded for life.

"And be sure to tell your father not to discuss certain topics while 'her nibs' is under his roof," Jackie cautioned Seán.

"What topics?" asked Aisling, whose inner detective was on red alert. Jackie's only response was an icy stare.

Now that she was with grandad in Eamhain, Aisling was determined to unravel some family secrets: why had no one told her that Bláithín, her grandmother, had disappeared without trace? Who were the *sídhe*? Where did they live? What did they look like?

Grandad, the oldest living person in Eamhain, was sitting by the fire putting the finishing touches to the speech he was going to make before setting the bonfire ablaze. It was beyond Aisling's wildest dreams to be here again this Hallowe'en. Last year was deadly fun: music, dancing, fireworks, a huge bonfire in the village square, a blazing firewall that stretched from McCormac's hardware store to Dún Gréine, and every man, woman and child out until the small hours of the morning when the bonfire embers were brought home for good luck.

"Will the *sídhe* be out and about tonight?" she asked, leaning forwards in her chair.

"Yes."

"In Eamhain?"

"Dún Gréine. That's their sacred space."

Dún Gréine was only a ten minute walk from Eamhain. Aisling had picnicked there with her dad. "What do they look like, grandad?"

He put his finger to his lips. "Better not be caught discussing the *sídhe*," he said, "or Meg will send you packing and I'll be in the dog house."

Aisling laughed. She knew that she and grandad, her buddy, would talk when the coast was clear. She'd tweeze the information from him later. A plan was forming in her mind to borrow a torch and some batteries from grandad's garden shed, go to Dún Gréine and ask the *sídhe* if *they* knew what had happened to Bláithín in 1965. Grandad must have read her thoughts. "The *sídhe*," he said with a heavy sigh, "inhabit an alluring parallel world. Keep your snoopy nose out of it or you'll find yourself sucked right in. Never, ever tamper or trifle with beings from other dimensions. Anyone who has trespassed on Dún Gréine lands on May eve or Hallowe'en has suffered the consequences."

"What consequences, grandad?"

He frowned, dropped the speech he was working on, glared at her and said: "The *sídhe* are always on the lookout for young ones like you to work for them below as nurses and midwives."

"I'm eleven years old, or have you forgotten?"

Grandad Aonghus stared into the fire, ignoring her comment. "If those leeches stick to you, you're marked for life."

"Leeches?"

"That dark-haired, unearthly beauty, the *leannán sídhe* loves, inspires and then abandons our finest poets, artists and writers. Once possessed by her, they live brilliant but brief lives. Yeats called her a blood-sucking vampire. She and her morbid sister, the *bean sídhe*, wreak havoc wherever they go. Dún Gréine is taboo tonight, right?"

"Ah! Don't worry, grandad. If I go below I'll bring along a needle and a spool of red thread, just like the one Ariadne gave to Theseus that got him out of the labyrinth." Aisling knew her Greek mythology and loved showing it off.

"A spool of thread might have worked for them, but it wouldn't fool our supernatural *sídhe* for a second," grandad informed her. "Young and old have been whisked away to the underworld by them, never to return. You don't want to learn the hard way like my own—" His voice trailed away.

"Your own—" Aisling asked, tilting her head, her eyes carefully scanning his careworn face.

"Doesn't matter," he muttered, staring into the fire. "Let's not look back. It's all in the past."

"What's in the past, grandad?"

He swung around in his chair, looked at her, his blue eyes boring holes into her very soul.

"Don't stir things up, Aisling. Leave well enough alone."

"But I don't understand."

He raised his blackthorn stick. "Stay away from Dún Gréine or your mother will never let you stay with us again. Do you hear me child? Do you hear me now?"

"What has she against you grandad?"

"You'll find out in good time," he said, his lips trembling. "Our bonfire and firewall will keep the *sídhe* away from us tonight."

"We have a firewall on our school computer to keep out spam."

"And we in Eamhain have carefully adapted the military firewall to defend ourselves against the *sídhe* at Hallowe'en and May eve," he said. "I'm no authority on computers but I know what spam is, and you are spam as far as the *sídhe* are concerned. They could delete you in the blink of an eye."

Her mouth quivered and he changed the subject.

"We're designing fire gates for next year. Maybe your Mr Microsoft would do the honours at the unveiling."

"Fire gates?" She brightened up.

"We constantly upgrade our defences against *bobaireacht na sídhe.*"

"*Bobaireacht na sídhe?*"

"Hoodwinkery."

"What's that?"

"I thought you Dubliners knew everything."

"I'm not allowed talk about the *sídhe* at home," Aisling explained.

"*Bobaireacht na sídhe* or hoodwinkery, Aisling, is an ancient science which can only be studied in UUI."

"Never heard of it."

"UUI, Aisling, is the Underworld University of Ireland. Elementary studies in year one are deceit, deviousness and devilment. There are as many grades in the mastery of hood-winkery, which is as old as time itself, as there are stars in the sky. A *lios* is a hive of many secrets."

"What's a *lios*, grandad?"

"It's a communal home where the *sídhe* live."

"Like a beehive?"

"Yes, just like the beehive at the bottom of our garden. Go near a *lios* and you'll get badly stung. Your dad told me you were hospitalized in the States last summer with a whopper of a bee-sting. Isn't that so?"

"Yes, but let's not look back," said Aisling, quoting grandad's own words.

"If the little *lios* men and *lios* women catch you interfering in their festivities tonight, they'll take you away with them, Miss Smarty Bum. You keep the word spam in mind and stay on our side of the firewall. Now fetch me some more logs for the fire, like a good girl."

"Sure grandad. I've just one more question. Is it true that if you catch a *lios* man's cap, its owner must obey your every command?"

"Who told you that?"

"Miss Moore said that a *sidhe* cap is a passport to their world. It's a kind of blessing."

"Aisling, mark my words: the *sidhe* blessing is often a curse, and the *sidhe* curse a blessing. Now what about those logs you promised me?"

Aisling brought in some logs and put them on the hearth.

"That reminds me," she said, "I'd better head off and gather some crackly sticks for tonight. See you later."

And away she ran like the wind to the woods.

Chapter Two

Rowanberries, bonfires, and firewalls

Aisling sped up the road to Coill na bPúcaí, hopped over the dry-stone wall, stooped to pick some dry twigs near a tall oak tree, and noticed to her surprise and delight that she was in a mushroom circle which entitled her to make a wish. Just as she did, she heard a rustle in the undergrowth, swung around ever so quickly just in time to glimpse a tiny shadow disappearing from view. Who or what was it? She shivered with excitement but decided not to investigate. It was too soon to go below. Instead, she scooped up as many twigs as her arms could carry and raced back to the cottage and the smell of Meg's baking.

"Guess what grandad? When I was in the woods I think I saw one of the little—" but she never finished the sentence as Meg came in from the kitchen with currant scones, raspberry jam and a jug of fresh cream.

"Eat your fill," said grandad, as she tucked into them. "It'll be a long night."

"Magic!" she spluttered through a mouthful of scone. "I can't wait!"

Meg poured the tea. "Thanks, Meg. Have you more of these scrumptious scones for the Hallowe'en party?"

"Yes, and I'm looking forward to your grandad's speech. He has spent days working on it."

"The *slua sídhe* are leaving their dwelling places in the underworld now," said grandad in a hushed tone of voice. "Coaches of *lios* men and *lios* women, drawn by *sídhe* horses, are galloping across land and sky. *Curracha sídhe*, packed to capacity, are crossing rivers and streams on their way to Dún Gréine."

"Let's make tracks," suggested Aisling.

"Not yet," said grandad in a firm tone of voice. "Sit by the window. Watch, listen and, above all, be patient. Tune in to every huff, puff, and whistle of the north wind. When the leaves stop swirling and the huffs, puffs, and squalls die down, then and only then, will we leave."

Aisling positioned herself by the window and pressed her nose to the glass. It was pitch black outside except for the crescent moon which stalked the night sky. Some stray ivy leaves tapped against the window pane, others just fluttered by.

"How will I recognize the *sídhe*?" she called over her shoulder.

"Watch for flashes of light. Their horsemen carry their heads in their right hands as lanterns and listen for the galloping of hooves and the lashing of whips."

Aisling winced. The *sídhe* world was as terrifying as it was irresistible.

"How long before I see them?" she asked after what seemed like an eternity.

"The *sídhe* materialize and de-materialize at will. A novice like you can't expect miracles." Grandad reached for his overcoat and hat.

"It's toffee apple time," he said. "One is enough. We don't want a repeat of last year when your eyes were bigger than your belly."

He handed over her red bomber-jacket and scarf.

"It's bitter outside," he added.

Aisling picked up her bundle of twigs and fingered the torch and batteries in her pocket.

"We're off," grandad shouted into the kitchen.

"Be right there after you," said Meg, "just as soon as I've tidied up here."

They took the shortcut down Foxglove Lane, grandad's yellow torch lighting the way through Fairy Hollow. They passed the tall oak tree and the rowanberry bushes. Grandad stooped to pick some berries.

"Eat," he said. "The berries are ripe. Look at the pentagram clearly marked on them."

"What's a pentagram?" asked Aisling, eating a handful of the berries.

"It's a five-pointed star shape, a symbol of the five elements: earth, air, fire, water and spirit. You can draw a pentagram in five straight strokes," he explained. "Rowanberries are the food of the gods and offer us, mere mortals, protection against *bobaireacht na sídhe*."

They cut through O'Flaherty's cornfield and headed down Bluebell Walk towards Eamhain. Aisling, her lips pressed tightly together, pondered her plan for later on. She daren't blurt it out accidentally.

"Are you sorry you're not in Dublin trick or treating?" Grandad was concerned at her silence.

"You can't be serious!" Aisling wrinkled up her nose in disdain. She didn't envy her Dublin friends their Hallowe'en goodies, horror videos and sleepovers. The prospect of meeting the *sídhe*, terrifying as it was, surpassed even roasted chestnuts back home. Here in Eamhain, Hallowe'en was celebrated in the old tradition. She drooled in anticipation of tonight's toffee apples and gingerbread men, and shivered with excitement at the thought of the fire-pit and firewall which would light up the October sky.

Grandad nudged her. "Penny for your thoughts, girl," he said.

She laughed. "Get a life! Even Eamhain deals in euros now."

He chuckled. "Shhh! There's music in the air. The square is packed already."

Sure enough it was. The village councillors and the Lord Mayor, wearing her chain of office, were deeply engrossed in conversation. Doctor and Polly Pollock were chatting with Father John. The ever-so-snooty Sheehan family from the big house, whose children went to school in Brussels, were *actually* mixing with the locals. Sylvester Sheehan must have had a mid-term assignment on "ancient traditions" as he was writing in a red notebook. Painted lanterns made by the national school children hung with colourful balloons from the lamp posts. Carnival lights festooned the trees. Stacks of logs, broken chairs, stools, and everything flammable or past its use-by date were stacked beside the fire-pit. Tar-filled stone troughs lined the main street all the way to Dún Gréine. Soon the carefully selected beech and ash logs would be set alight in them, creating the firewall.

On a raised platform in front of the Poitín Still, the local amateur drama group was staging a mock battle, armed with slash hooks and pitch forks. Fireworks and bangers followed. Then, eight Irish dancers, accompanied by box, bodhrán and fiddle players, did a reel through skipping ropes which had been dipped in blazing tar. They put *Riverdance* to shame. Jugglers expertly hurled flaming spears at each other, over the heads of the gawking villagers. Everyone was invited to cross barefooted over the beds of red-hot coals. Only the stalwarts accepted the challenge. Then the brassy pealing of the village bell silenced one and all. Grandad Aonghus left Aisling's side and walked over to the fire-pit. He was handed a flaming torch and just like the torch bearer at the Olympic Games, he held it ceremoniously in his right hand.

You could hear a blackberry drop as he said: "Dear villagers, it is a great honour for me to light our *Samhain* bonfire in time-honoured tradition on this Hallowe'en night. Our ancestors knew and appreciated how the sun helps the crops grow. They noticed how it began to fade at the end of autumn when the harvest was gathered. Once their stock of both animal and grain was safely stored in winter shelters, they quenched the home fires, came to this square where a huge bonfire was lit. We now follow the example set by them long ago. On this night, they thanked the sun for its warmth and asked it to return when winter was over. Then they partied in style. After the festivities, each villager brought home a burning stick or an ember from the bonfire, from which the home-fire was lit once again. I now—"

Aisling shifted from foot to foot knowing that she had to make her move as, in a moment or so, grandad would torch the kindling in the fire-pit and in the gutters which went all the way to Dún Gréine. She slipped away from the enraptured audience and ran up the main street as fast as her legs could carry her, her torch lighting up the road ahead. Her heart pounded as she heard the sound of crackling wood. She knew the fire was catching up on her, its flames licking and hissing close to her feet. She didn't dare look behind as she ran through the open gate into Dún Gréine. Phew! Just in the nick of time.

She ran past the dolmen where she and dad had enjoyed a picnic when the fairy fingers (dad called them foxgloves) were in bloom, paused for a minute at the ancient sun fort while she got her breath back, and then crept beneath the hawthorn bush which rustled a little as she sat down and made herself comfortable. Sparks and flames lit up the night sky.

The flat ground in front of the hawthorn bush was in fact where the *sídhe* danced. Would she see them in their parallel world? She would, if the wish she made earlier in the mushroom circle came true. She sat ever so still, hardly daring to breathe. As the village bell chimed, enchanting music wafted all about. It sounded to her like bluebells ringing and soprano gypsy-moths humming. She was unaware that the paths were thronged with *lios* men and *lios* women rushing headlong to dance until the small hours. A sudden burst of wind blasted against her. She closed her eyes and wished that, when she opened them again, the audible would be visible. Her inner voice startled her with these words, "As your heart is in your dream, no request is too extreme."

The wind stopped. Something fluttered past. She reached up quickly and caught a tiny pointed emerald green cap with a gold, four-leafed clover embroidered on it. She trembled as the realization dawned on her that this was her passport below. Danger: *would she disappear without trace like her grandmother, Bláithín*—and opportunity—*could this be her passport below,* beckoned her in this moment. She pressed the little cap to her heart and, as she did, her

astonished eyes beheld countless swarms of little people swirling and twirling round and round, tumbling and somersaulting head over heels in time to *sídhe* music. A sturdy, two-foot tall fellow, with a face like a dried apple, spiky red hair, a long bushy beard and piercing green eyes, dressed in a leaf-green shirt, grey leather shorts, and black bootees, came forward.

"I'll have my cap back if you please," he said in a high-pitched voice.

Aisling gripped it firmly with clenched hands, Spock-eyed him, and in a firm tone of voice said, "Steady on there, don't come any closer."

The *lios* man stopped dead in his tracks. Mr Owl, the orchestra conductor, dropped his baton and the music and dancing stopped. The *lios* people muttered crossly amongst themselves and stared in fury at Aisling.

"Fetch me food and drink." She squared her shoulders, determined to stay in command of this once in a lifetime opportunity.

The green-eyed *lios* man hesitated momentarily before tucking his bushy beard into his belt and scurrying away.

"On! On with the music and dancing," she ordered.

The orchestra was joined by a host of butterflies who flapped their wings in G Major and a swarm of bumblebees who buzzed in B Minor and thousands more little *lios* people gave an energetic display of intricate footwork. Just before dawn, the larks made their first appearance and Mr Owl ticked them off for their late arrival. The *lios* man returned with exotic fruits, truffles and shells of sloe and haw juices on a gold dish which he put on Aisling's knees.

"Your name?" she asked.

"No name!" he answered with a scowl.

"No name?" repeated Aisling, "how strange."

"Names are unnecessary in the underworld," he said, his tone of voice matter of fact.

"In our world," she informed him, "everyone has a name. You'll answer to No-Name from now on."

He shrugged his shoulders.

The sun peeped above the horizon. The dancers stopped. Mr Owl dropped the baton once more and the orchestra, led off by the first nightingale, drifted away. A small trapdoor slid open in the ground. A wicker basket rose to the surface. Swarms of *lios* men and *lios* women jumped in. It took off downwards.

"What about you and me?" Aisling asked No-Name. "I'm going below, you know."

"*Leipreacháin, fir dearga,* and *cluricháin* ahead of No-Namers," he answered, as others jumped into the barrel and took off.

"*Cluricháin* and *fir dearga*?" "Underworld boozers and men in red, practical jokers of the *sídhe*, as you'll find out in time," No-Name answered.

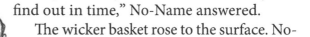

The wicker basket rose to the surface. No-Name stepped in, followed by Aisling. The door closed over. She shivered with excitement as the wicker basket went down to the centre of the earth. Plonk! It landed.

Chapter Three

In Forbidden Territory with a Strange Guide

Aisling woke up in a four poster bed under a fringed canopy. A diamond as big as a *sliotar* lit up the room and everything sparkled and shone like gold. These *sidhe* were rich, she reckoned. Silk clothes were laid out on the bedside chair, under which a pair of black, shiny, handmade shoes awaited her. She put them on and everything fitted perfectly. No-Name knocked on the door before entering with a trolley laden with berry juices, oat flakes, and nutty brown bread.

"Breakfast first, then class," he said.

"Class!" exclaimed Aisling, an expression of horror on her face.

"Safe Cross Code," No-Name replied.

"But Miss Moore has already done that with us," protested Aisling.

"Hmmm." No-Name, a man of few words, moved towards the door.

"Where are you going?"

"To inform Fionnbharr that you refuse to study our code."

"What then?"

"You'll get the royal boot out."

"Okay. You win." Aisling wasn't ready to leave the underworld just yet.

"Eat first," he ordered.

She polished off every tasty morsel and pushed the trolley aside. No-Name opened the lid of a miniature roll-top desk which contained a bowl of seeds, an acorn, a slate, a dice, flints, and some maps.

"Did I not hear you say Safe Cross Code class?" Aisling was perplexed.

"Correct. Take a seed of knowledge, chew it well, and then swallow," said No-Name.

"Can I have a glass of water?"

"Watering down knowledge is forbidden," said No-Name.

"But I must—"

"Opportunity lost." No-Name marked the slate with a bit of flint, stating: *Seed swallowing unsuccessful. Reason: student has attitude problem.*

He handed her the dice.

"At least I don't have to swallow this," she exclaimed with relief. "Do I throw it or what?"

"Toss it."

"What's this game called?"

"Shape-shifting is not a game. Toss an even number and change into any animal of your choice, toss an uneven number and I choose for you."

"That's crazy!"

He marked the slate again: *Shape-shifting: unsuccessful. Reason: negative attitude.*

No-Name spoke sternly. "Refuse map reading at your peril."

"I love map reading."

He spread one of the maps on a table. "Find the entrance to Dún Gréine," he instructed.

The markings on the map puzzled her.

"Look for a sun symbol above a stone fort."

She peered at the map. "Here!" she exclaimed, thrilled, "near the hawthorn bush. It marks the entrance to the underworld, doesn't it?"

"Yes."

"Are these Cruachan and Tara?" she asked, pointing at two separate hawthorn bushes on grassy mounds.

"Correct. The entrances to our No-Namedoms are all clearly marked."

"Your *what*doms?"

"A king has a kingdom, and a No-Namer has a No-Namedom," he said, marking the slate as follows: *Level 1: map reading successful.*

He opened out a second map entitled "Underworld". Aisling peered at the seven symbols on it. She named sun, moon and star quickly.

"Name the other heavenly bodies," he instructed.

"On this underworld map?" she asked disbelievingly.

"The heavenly bodies are *here*, Aisling, their reflection above."

"You can't be serious?" Her tone of voice was scornful.

No-Name reached for his slate and flint. Before he had time to mark it, Aisling asked in a more respectful tone of voice, "Here? The heavenly bodies are here?"

"Your world is just the evident part of our hidden world: the tip of our iceberg, so to speak."

"That's mad!" He pointed to the map again. "Do you recognize any other planets?"

"Yes, Venus and Mars," she said, after some time in deep concentration.

She recognized them from the curious intricate geometric patterns which were etched overnight last year, in O'Flaherty's cornfield. He was convinced that UFOs had set up an observatory on his land. A starfish formation had appeared on mid-summer's day, followed by two circles with attachments, Venus and Mars, which crop circle experts from New York had identified. The Venus circle had an upside-down cross underneath, and the Mars one had an arrow sticking out from the top right hand side. Aisling didn't recognize the remaining two heavenly bodies on No-Name's map.

No-Name pointed to a symbol ♃ that resembled the number four. "Jupiter," he said, "and this one," pointing to a symbol ♄ that resembled the letter *h* with a bar on top, "is Saturn."

"I'll recognize them if they appear in O'Flaherty's cornfield," she said.

"Map reading complete," said No-Name. He marked the slate. "Now repeat in order: sun, moon, star, Jupiter, Venus, Saturn and Mars."

"Sun, moon, star, Venus, Saturn, Mars and—Jupiter."

No sooner said than Aisling did a somersault and landed on her head.

"Turn me round, No-Name."

He spun her around, clockwise.

"Not like that!" she protested. "Turn me upside-down."

She did a 360-degree somersault.

"Put me back on my feet," she roared.

"Not until you name the heavenly bodies in their correct order."

"That's so stupid!" she shouted in anger. "My head hurts and I feel weak. What's happening to me?"

"Your negative thoughts and words have lowered your frequency which affects your well-being. We, the *sídhe*, vibrate at an all time high frequency."

"Why celebrate May eve and Hallowe'en in our low frequency world then?" she inquired, a twinkle in her eye.

"For your benefit, not ours," he answered. "We, the *sídhe*, play a very important role in your lives and we are always on the lookout for a potential *idirghabhálaí*."

"What's that?"

"An *idirghabhalaí* is a go-between. Your grandmother, Bláithín, was one of our best. *She* could recite the heavenly bodies perfectly."

"I'll give it another go."

Aisling, who didn't like to be outdone, recited them in perfect order and found herself instantly upright.

The class came to an end with the sounding of a gong. "The banquet is ready. Follow me," instructed No-Name as he tucked his bushy beard into his belt. They went down a long curving rock-cut corridor. A small arched doorway led into a five columned banqueting room. Weird animal and bird paintings adorned its ceiling. Throngs of servants, dressed in long, white linen coats and open sandals, balanced plates laden with fish, fowl, fruit, and fine wines on their heads. They served a motley gathering of *sídhe*, seated at long oak tables. Aisling was later to discover, to her horror, that they were, in fact, human children who had been plucked from their homes and transported to the underworld, from which they could never escape, as they had partaken of *sídhe* food and wine without due protection. Here, stunned into silence, they meekly carried out their tasks.

Sitting on his throne at the top table, which was covered with a white linen cloth, was the Ard Rí, Fionnbharr. The queen, Oonagh, sat on his right. No-Name led Aisling directly to Fionnbharr, who gestured to her to sit on the vacant chair beside him.

"How are your lessons going?" he asked. Aisling wasn't quite sure how to answer this question. If she didn't answer truthfully, there would very likely be some kind of a backlash.

"Er, very interesting, indeed," she replied. "No-Name is an excellent teacher."

Fionnbharr smiled and said, "Indeed! Welcome to our wonderland."

"Welcome to our wonderland," echoed the *sídhe*, "welcome to our wonderland."

Aisling looked around at all the smiling faces. She looked over her shoulder at No-Name. He, too, was smiling. She glanced over at Oonagh, who had a face on her, as grandad would say, that would curdle milk. Aisling concluded that she was given to mood swings just like her own mother, Jackie.

Oonagh nudged Fionnbharr and then whispered in his ear. His smile changed to a frown. The *sídhe* followed suit. Aisling asked ever so politely, "Is something wrong?"

"Everything," he replied.

"Everything," echoed all the *sidhe*, "everything."

Aisling was shocked. "A moment ago you were all smiling. You said I was welcome to your wonderland."

"And so you were, and now you're not," he said.

"And so you were, and now you're not," echoed all the *sidhe*. "And so you were and now you're not."

Aisling turned around to No Name. "What's the matter?" she asked, her furrowed brow indicating her unease. He turned away.

Fionnbharr answered the question. "Oonagh doesn't trust you."

An outraged Aisling protested, "I've done nothing wrong."

"Oonagh reckons you're a mischief-making smart-alec."

Aisling pointed to No-Name's cap. "This is my green-card, like it or not."

Oonagh whispered in Fionnbharr's ear again, this time audibly. "She and Bláithín are two of a kind. She is to be kept within limits and under surveillance at all times. I'll set her an IQ test and then we'll review the situ—" Her voice faded.

Aisling was secretly thrilled to hear her name linked to Bláithín's: proof positive that she too had been here.

She smiled inwardly; IQ tests, riddles, and puzzles were right up her street.

"I propose a toast to Dana, our mother goddess," Fionnbharr raised his goblet on high, clinked Oonagh's and Aisling's goblet.

"A toast to Dana, our mother goddess," echoed all the *sidhe*. "A toast to Dana, our mother goddess."

"Where might I find Dana?" Aisling asked.

Oonagh curled her lip at her. "Dana doesn't mix with riffraff missy," she answered.

"On with the banquet," said Fionnbharr. The *lios* people ate and drank their fill and when the meal was over and the tables pushed aside, they leapt onto the floor, jigging and reeling and

whooping it up. The servants and No-Name joined in the fun. Fionnbharr jived with Oonagh. Only Aisling didn't dance. She would have loved to, but she wasn't asked.

The evening's fun finished with the tolling of a bell. No-Name escorted Aisling back to her room where she slept soundly in her four poster bed until morning.

Chapter Four

Gods of Chaos, gods of Light, jesters, and a big black hole

Settling in well with the underground folk, Aisling continued her studies with No-Name and excelled in map reading. They made daily excursions into the underworld which had meadows, lakes teeming with fish, hills, mountains, and islands. It irritated her that No-Name, like a tracker dog, was always hot on her heels. She felt ready to venture on alone. In the passageways she often heard the sound of swift flowing streams but, as yet, she couldn't see them. No-Name told her that, although she had *sidhe* sight, she wasn't yet in tune with *all* the frequencies of the underworld.

One day, walking by the seashore she saw a man, who looked like one of the ancient druids in grandad's old school history book, in silent meditation at the entrance to a cave. No-Name said he was very wise and had knowledge of past, present, and future.

"I'll ask him to read my palm," she said, making her way over to him.

"No, you won't," said No-Name, pulling her back. "Even I have to make an appointment to speak with a *saoi* and your antennae are not sufficiently fine-tuned to our vibrations to converse with superior beings. Some of your great artists, writers and painters did raise their vibrations sufficiently to draw inspiration from us. William Butler Yeats tuned into *our* poetry, blind Turlough O'Carolan played *our* timeless tunes on his harp and the artist, Jim Fitzpatrick, at only eight years of age, received a vision of *our* world which he has recreated in his masterpieces."

"Grandad Aonghus says that the *leannán sídhe* and her morbid sister, the bean *sídhe*, are leeches who suck the energy out of our artists."

"Not true, Aisling. Your artists, once bereft of our inspiration, lose the will to live, pine away and die."

"Can't wait to tell grandad," said Aisling who intended to write it up later in her notebook.

They came to a meadow of wild flowers and rushes. Aisling plucked a rush and felt a surge of adrenalin as it transformed into a horse and arched its back, allowing them both to mount; it then cantered to a nearby orchard where Aisling and No-Name slid down and the horse reverted to rush form. To her astonishment, a juicy apple which she plucked was instantly replaced by a larger and juicier one. No-Name told her that underworld herbalists used these fruits in the manufacture of cures.

"Have they a cure for arthritis?" she asked. "Meg suffers with her hip."

"Of course," replied No-Name. "Every blade of grass that grows, every flower, fruit, plant, and herb has within it a cure."

"Why do the *sídhe* need cures?" she asked.

"We don't," he replied, "but you folk do. At night we pass our cures on to you in dreams, and, by day, we slip them into the spaces between your thoughts. We have given our cures to Marie Curie, Louis Pasteur and Bach who invented the now famous flower remedies."

"So! What about Meg's arthritis?" asked Aisling.

"When we get to the herbal *lios*, you can ask Darach about his arthritis cure," said No-Name, "but we will head back now as we mustn't be late for the evening's entertainment."

He whittled a hazel rod with a flint stone and out of the shavings emerged an awesome bird, not unlike a golden eagle. They sat on it and it soared up on the back of the wind and flew them to the doorway of the banqueting room. Fionnbharr and Oonagh awaited them. Aisling sat, as usual, on the vacant chair beside Fionnbharr who said that he was looking forward to the magicians and storytellers, and that he hoped she would enjoy the evening. Oonagh smirked.

Obnoxious old hag! Aisling ignored her and turned to Fionnbharr.

"I love magic and stories," she declared.

"Our storytellers will tell of the great awakening at the dawn of time, Aisling, when the Fomorians and the Tuatha Dé Danann, gods of chaos and of light, fought the mighty battle of Moytura using hurleys as weapons. Hurling is still very popular here."

"Do you play by our rules?" she asked.

Fionnbharr and Oonagh sniggered, as did all the *sídhe*.

"The rules are ours, Aisling," Fionnbharr corrected her, as he winked conspiratorially at Oonagh. "Maybe we'll organize a special hurling match during Aisling's stay with us and give her a bird's eye view of it."

"Thank you so much, I'm looking forward to it already," Aisling said politely.

Oonagh stifled a snort.

Weird or what! Aisling was puzzled. She intended to record these titbits of information on hurling in her notebook. Oonagh, during the main course of wild boar, served on a bed of brown wild rice, slipped a note to Fionnbharr, who nudged Aisling and placed it in her hand without comment. She took a quick peek at it. "*Nota bene*, read tomorrow, *nota bene*." Was this the IQ test? She longed to read it right now, but knew it would be unwise to do so. She slipped her foot out of her shoe and tucked Oonagh's note into it. She wondered if Bláithín, too, had been given this same test before becoming a go-between. Aisling also wanted to become a *sídhe* lore expert. Fionnbharr told her he was impressed with her most recent study reports and that he hoped all her dreams would be fulfilled. She was so thrilled at these words that she failed to notice the arrival of storytellers and magicians, the latter in gold embroidered black cloaks, muttering strange-sounding incantations and waving wisps of straw in the air. A hush descended over the banqueting hall and Aisling's sixth sense warned her of impending danger.

A bolt of lightning struck the oak table, which groaned and shuddered before everything went black as pitch. She looked for Fionnbharr, Oonagh, and No-Name, but couldn't see them. She was alone. Loud wailings and ear-splitting screams sounded all around. Aisling's blood ran cold. A deep rasping voice said: "In the beginning, before the dawn of time, the universe was dark, cold and empty. Light particles appeared. A big black hole ravenously sucked so many of them into itself that it exploded and the little specks of light escaped into the darkness above forming themselves into dazzling constellations.

CORK CITY LIBRARIES

The black hole yowled. It summoned the Fomorians, gods of chaos, whose empire is under the sea, to a meeting. The Fomorians pledged to help them destroy all light. The constellations summoned the Tuatha Dé Danann, gods of light, whose empire is in the heavens, to a meeting. They mapped out the sky taking care to position the stars far out of reach of the black hole."

Wisps of straw touched Aisling's face. A gaping abyss opened at her feet, sucking her chair downwards. A slimy fire-breathing muscular creature coiled up her legs, excreting foul-smelling mucous droplets as it looped itself around her body. She let out a blood-curdling scream. Every time she exhaled, the brute tightened its grip, almost squeezing the very life out of her, its teeth leaving puncture wounds in her throat, forcing her to take short convulsive breaths any one of which could have been her last gasp. Grandad Aonghus' warnings about *bobaireacht na sídhe* flashed before her. What a fool she was to think she could trust, let alone out-smart, them.

She was losing consciousness when a myriad of stars formed a halo around her. In the dim light she noticed Fionnbharr and Oonagh shaking with mirth and the *lios* people rocking with laughter in the aisles. As she looked over her shoulder at a chuckling No-Name, Aisling realized that once again, the *sídhe* were a step ahead.

The magicians and storytellers bowed low. Fionnbharr beamed as he congratulated them. Everyone clapped, except Aisling who realized that here in the underworld she was nothing more than a puppet on a string.

"We shall have to educate Aisling in the art of elusion," Fionnbharr said, winking at Oonagh. A perplexed Aisling wished she had a dictionary to hand. What, she wondered, were they on about?

"Don't be such a spoil sport," Oonagh responded. She turned and eye-balled Aisling. "It's the Law of Hades here," she said, with a twisted smile. "She who plays with fire shall have her little fingers burnt."

For the first time since her arrival in the underworld Aisling longed to be home in dreary old Dublin with Jackie and Seán.

She heaved a sigh of relief when No-Name escorted her back to her room.

Chapter Five

A blackthorn stick
and an unfinished book

"Great fun last night, wasn't it?" No-Name remarked the following morning.

"It was a nightmare," Aisling replied. "That she-devil set me up."

"What did you expect? You're an outsider, here on sufferance, light entertainment for us immortals. Write that in your notebook with an asterisk."

"I'm so tired," said Aisling. "Any chance we could skip class and go sightseeing instead?"

"I'll ask Fionnbharr," said No-Name.

Something about the way he strode out compelled Aisling to glance down at her shoes. What was it about shoes? Oh yes. She remembered: Oonagh's note. Shivering with excitement, she reached down, took it out and read as follows: SC: Journey's End: 2N2R1S1N1S = Exit. The key-shaped symbol which outlined the SC and the footprint which outlined the letters puzzled her. She placed the IQ test on the desk.

"When did you get that?" No-Name asked on his return.

"Last night. Do you know what it means?"

"I really can't say."

"Can't or won't?"

He didn't answer. Instead, he lifted up a little blackthorn stick from the desk. "Lessons must continue," he said. "Follow me."

I'll crack this IQ test with or without you, Aisling resolved, stuffing the note into her pocket and following No-Name down a long tunnel. The ground was embedded with sapphires, emeralds, and rubies. She jumped from stone to stone. It was magical. No-Name tucked his beard into his belt, raised the blackthorn stick, and tapped the tunnel walls. Instantly, an army of flowers sprang out, arranged themselves in rows, and stood to attention like soldiers. No-Name clicked his heels and walked up like a general inspecting his troops, pointing out a displaced petal or a speck of dust on a leaf. Once the inspection was complete, he tapped the tunnel walls once more and the flowers retreated. Aisling was spellbound.

No-Name handed her the blackthorn stick.

"Here," he said, "it's yours."

"For keeps?" she asked.

"For keeps," he replied. "Practise using it often. When it responds to your wishes, you will know that you are growing in our image and likeness. Believe and receive its powers."

"Gee! Thanks No-Name. Can I have a go at tapping the tunnel walls?"

"You can try."

Aisling tapped. A single flower popped out its head and retreated ever so quickly. She tapped again. Two flowers emerged and stood to attention before retreating.

"Grandad has a blackthorn stick," Aisling informed him, "for protection against the *sídhe*. He found it near the great dolmen at Dún Gréine in a bed of purple foxgloves. It's long and stout."

"Mmm, Bláithín had one too as far as I remember."

"You met her?"

"Yes, but I wasn't her guide. Why do you ask?"

"Because I knew nothing about her until I came across the Ó Dubhghaill family tree chart in dad's desk, along with a newspaper clipping which detailed her mysterious disappearance."

"Bláithín was a go-between and a *bean feasa*," No-Name informed her.

"A *bean* what?"

"A *bean feasa* forges links between our world and yours, manages internal and external communications and helps create and maintain a positive image of us."

"Did she know all your secrets?"

"No-one will ever know them all, Aisling. Bláithín, I understand, was writing a book about the *sídhe*. It had a silver cover."

"Maybe she disappeared down here on one of her trips or maybe the wicked witch Oonagh cast a spell on her."

"I wouldn't take that tone when you're talking about Oonagh. The walls around here have ears. Bláithín had her own No-Namer. He may have the answer to your question."

"I bet you anything that Oonagh had something to do with her disappearance."

"Oonagh's business is hers and hers alone," said No-Name, his nostrils flaring momentarily. "You would be foolhardy to cross her."

"What else have you heard about my grandmother, Bláithín?"

"She was active in Eamhain's folklore society, wrote a column about us for the local gazette which was widely read and she was a regular visitor here."

"Do you think I'm like her? She went missing in 1965."

"You have an enquiring mind, you take notes, and," he added with a twisted smile, "you both were cap-napped at Hallowe'en." He threw back his head and laughed.

"You mean kidnapped."

"I said cap-napped."

"What? You mean we were deliberately lured here?"

"You hardly think it was all down to luck and midnight festivals?" he sniggered, as he tugged on his beard. "It's time to try the blackthorn stick again."

"About this cap-napping—"

"Forget I said it," said No-Name. "It's time to try the black-thorn stick again."

"But—"

No-Name took out his slate and flint. "Back to work or—"

Aisling took out the blackthorn stick and to her great delight a row of flowers sprang out when she tapped on the tunnel wall. She inspected them as No-Name had done, straightening stray petals and drooping stalks, and brushing away specks of dust. The flowers retreated when the inspection was complete. Practice was the secret to success, she reflected. Soon it was time to return. Aisling hoped to impress Fionnbharr tonight when he quizzed her on the day's lesson. She took another look at Oonagh's IQ test. SC = Security Code; that was easy, but what did the letters stand for? The answer struck her like a bolt from the blue. Of course! The two Ns were for sun and moon. The code comprised the last letter of each of the heavenly bodies, in their correct sequence. She had to leave her footprint in each of the seven zones before she would exit the under-world. Was grandmother Bláithín still trapped in one of them? The gong rang.

"Banquet time," announced No-Name. "Come on; mustn't keep Fionnbharr waiting."

"Be right there after you," said Aisling taking a last look at the IQ test.

She walked down the tunnel after No-Name, hopping from one precious stone to another. A huge topaz stone shaped like a sunflower glowed in the dusky light. She jumped on it with both feet and it started to revolve clockwise, just like Meg's musical ballerina on the top of her jewellery box. It was moving so fast, she had to be careful not to fall off. She knew she had to watch her step. Yippee! She had cracked the code. At last, it slowed down to a standstill. Seven streams of light radiated from the sunflower. One of them pointed straight ahead. Aisling decided to follow this stream of light. Everywhere was shrouded in an amber glow, just like the colour of O'Flaherty's cornfield at the end of summer. Would she ever see it again, or was there a column in the *Evening Herald* saying that she was missing, presumed dead, just like Bláithín?

Chapter Six

An Ogham map,
a treasure trove,
and a hurling champion

"**W**ho are you and what are you doing here?" Aisling swung around but saw no-one.

"And might I ask where are you?" she retorted.

"Here!" Someone tipped her on the shoulder. "Hi! I'm Fachtna Ó hAilpín. Shhh!"

A tall, scared looking, pale-faced, black-haired, brown-eyed boy, about her own age, put his finger to his lips.

"Shhh! Please don't make a sound. Maebh, Fionnbharr and Oonagh's daughter, is due back any moment now. She and her gang had better not catch you here or they'll take you hostage too, or worse."

"Maebh must be just like her mother," remarked Aisling.

"You've met Oonagh?"

"Yes, it's a long story."

"Hey! Maybe you know the way out. Where did you get that cap?"

"In Dún Gréine, on Hallowe'en night."

"You're so lucky. If only I had one I wouldn't go hungry," said Fachtna. "I have to survive on what little the magpie

37

brings here to this treasure *lios* from our world. If I eat *sídhe* food I'll be trapped here forever like the servants. Have you seen them in their long white linen coats? They're almost institutionalized. The more *sídhe* food they eat, the less they remember about their former lives."

"My grandad and I ate lots of rowanberries on our way to Eamhain, so I'm doubly protected."

"Is he here too?" asked Fachtna.

"Are you joking? My grandad doesn't trust the *sídhe*."

"He's dead right! They're a step ahead of us all the time. Don't lose that cap or you're in deadly trouble."

"I won't. It's great to talk to someone normal and to be rid of No-Name for a while, he's so intense."

"Where is he?"

"He's probably at Fionnbharr's banquet. That place gives me the shivers."

"It's scary here too."

"Why? Is Maebh a bit of a dragon?"

"Don't wait to find out, unless you want to be tied to a feather duster for the rest of your life. Cross her and she'll have you locked up for life in Manannán, the god of the sea's dungeons. Call your No-Name and ask him to take you out of here."

"I'll think about it. My name is Aisling, by the way."

"Please leave now," Fachtna gave her a little push.

"So, you came here with a feather duster! I'm tickled pink," Aisling laughed out loud.

"It's no laughing matter," said Fachtna. "I'm a champion hurler. By the way, if you ever escape, don't tell anyone you saw Fachtna Ó hAilpín of the famous hurling clan feather dusting in the underworld, or I'll never live it down, on or off the pitch."

"What brought you here?"

"Cúchulainn was a champion hurler. I was looking for his golden *sliotar* in Cruachan woods, when things backfired badly." Fachtna looked nervously over his shoulder. "I'd better get back to work. It's bad enough here without being caught slacking."

"I take it you didn't find it, not that I'd have expected you to."

"I did too. Follow me."

Aisling followed him down the passageway into a gallery filled with treasures. Fachtna pointed to the low ceiling where hanging from one of the oak beams in a silver mesh hammock was a golden sliotar.

"Cúchulainn's?" she asked, wide-eyed.

"Yes. Now go." He gave her another push.

"I've only just got here. Relax. I can call No-Name anytime. So you're a champion hurler?"

"Yes." He proudly puffed out his chest. "You are addressing the captain of Cruachan Juniors, this year's national champions. My hobby is collecting unusual *sliotair*."

"Would never have guessed," Aisling said with an impish grin as she looked up at the silver mesh hammock containing Cúchulainn's golden ball. "How many have you then?"

"A few," answered Fachtna, looking around anxiously.

"Any antique?"

"Yes. My grandad found an ancient *sliotar* in the Bog of Allen and my neighbour, Sean Ó Croinín, gave me a Christy Ring cowhide one from the 1940s."

"Hey! It's an Aladdin's Cave!" said Aisling, looking at the crystal cabinets filled with bracelets, torcs, and gold fibulas, and the bronze latticed windows which let in underworld light that shone on the black marble, diamond-studded floor.

"Tread lightly on the heavenly bodies underfoot," said Fachtna. "You're standing on the night sky, all the planets and the eighty-eight constellations."

"It's a mad place, the underworld, isn't it?" Aisling's eye was drawn to a silver and yew book shrine, not unlike the one she had seen in the National Museum. An open, richly ornamented calfskin book reminded her of the *Book of Kells* which she had seen in Trinity College.

"A boy of twelve named Seán, who will one day become a world famous archaeologist, is destined to find this book and shrine in Carraig an Phortaigh, near Crossmolina, his home place," Fachtna told her.

"How will he know it's there?" she asked.

"He will dream of its whereabouts," said Fachtna.

"Will he hand it over to the National Museum?" she asked.

"Hope so," said Fachtna. "There are treasures here brought to Ireland at the dawn of civilization. Maebh has charge of the sword of Lugh and the Daghda's harp. They were brought here by the Tuatha Dé Danann."

"Wow! Can I see them?"

"Later. Must dust now," Fachtna said, taking one of the many feather dusters that were around the place.

"I'll help," offered Aisling.

Fachtna hesitated. "Promise you'll vanish if Maebh appears."

"I'll keep out of her sight," said Aisling, proceeding to lightly dust some gold and ivory chessmen. "Is chess popular here?" she asked.

"It originated in the underworld. Fionnbharr is the undefeated champion of the *sídhe* universe, a grandmaster. *Sídhe* chess contestants come here each year for inter *lios* competitions and Manannán, the god of the sea, another chess grandmaster, presents the winner's trophy. Maebh is a great friend of Fand, his wife. By the way, we use gossamer cloths on gold," Fachtna said, handing over one. He pressed a little emerald bell on the wall. "Just calling the *sídhe* servants to help," he explained.

Swarms of *lios* servants appeared and ran around the room with bees-wax polish for the precious woods, and special dips for the torcs, lunulas, and precious stones. They were accompanied as they polished and dusted by harpists, fiddlers and drummers who played and sang working songs. The *sídhe* believe that music lightens the workload. Fachtna put one of the *sídhe* servants on duty in case Maebh made an appearance.

"How come you were looking for Cúchulainn's sliotar?" asked Aisling. "My grandad Senan and a guy named Aonghus, found an old document in Garvan's fort near Cruachan, when they were boys."

"That's my grandad's name," Aisling said interrupting him. "Bet you anything they were boyhood friends." Her imagination, as usual, was working overtime. "So what exactly was in the document?"

"Neither of them had the faintest idea because it was written in Ogham."

"What's Ogham?"

"It's a series of strokes meeting or crossing a centre line, a bit like the markings on a totem pole. It's a secret language and goes back a long time. The druids may have used it as a silent language, placing their fingers against an imaginary centre line down their chest to communicate with each other. Grandad Senan showed it to the headmaster of Cruachan national school but he couldn't make head nor tail of it. So grandad put it aside and forgot all about it, until last Easter when I stumbled across it."

"I'm a bit of a snoop myself. How did *you* manage to read the ancient markings?"

"I photocopied it and went to our local library where I found a book on Ogham. From the drawings and Ogham markings I figured out that Cúchulainn's *sliotar* was embedded in an oak tree at the fort of Cruachan. Cúchulainn spent a lot of time in Cruachan when he was young."

"And—"

Fachtna looked over his shoulder nervously.

"No sight or sound of herself," Aisling reassured him.

"On May eve, I filled a basket with wild garlic and oysters from the river bedrock and set out for Cruachan woods with

high hopes that I might bribe the *sídhe* to let me see Cúchulainn's *sliotar*."

"Were you scared?"

Fachtna's face froze momentarily. "Grandad Senan warned me about the hound, as big and ferocious as a dinosaur, which roams the woods tearing limb from limb any misfortunate creature who crosses its path, and the *sídhe* mist that disorientates even the expert orienteer, and the *féar gortach* that gives you a hunger like the Great Famine."

"You sound like a real storyteller."

"Thanks for the compliment. Everyone in my family says I take after my grandad. He told me stories about Oisín in Tír na nÓg and Diarmuid and Gráinne."

"What was it like in Cruachan woods?"

"I may as well have been in a jungle. I couldn't see anything with the brambles and creepers everywhere so I plucked some hazel rods, knocked aside the briars and in that instant I saw a troop of horses with flowing manes, wearing silver bridles, drawing a bronze and gold chariot full to the brim with bronze shields and swords destined for this treasure *lios*. You can see them later, if you like."

Aisling didn't interrupt Fachtna as he was on a roll now, animated and un-self-conscious.

"A light breeze passed over me and another *slua* of horses galloped by, carrying a pewter vat of wine. Small, golden goblets dangled from it on little golden chains. I heard a tramp, tramp, tramping behind me. It was an elk, waving its huge antlers in the wind. Little *lios* men all elegantly dressed in red, velvet jackets, green trousers and buckled shoes sat astride, chatting nineteen to the dozen. I made sure not to look into its eyes, or I'd have spent the rest of my days as mad as a March hare. They were on their way to the May eve festivities. Next thing, I was hoisted up, sat in front of the *lios* men on the elk and brought deeper into the woods to where some *lios* women were waiting for them. 'We came across this young lad with a basket of garlic and oysters, walking on our pathway,' said one of the *lios* men. 'Where are they then?' enquired one of the *lios* women, 'they'll be nice and tasty with our evening meal.' I must have dropped them, I explained, realizing I no longer had them. 'Pity, as we're very partial to oysters and mussels too. So if you have no mother-earth delicacies for us, what brings you here?' asked one of the *lios* women. 'You're too young for the set-dancing when the veil that separates our worlds is lifted and the locals join us.' They seemed nice and friendly, so I thought it no harm to tell them the truth. Actually, I said, I was hoping to find Cúchulainn's *sliotar* and hand it over to our National Museum. There was a deadly silence. Seconds later, they all shrieked in one voice: 'Cúchulainn's *sliotar*! He wants Cúchulainn's *sliotar*!' With a glint in her eye, the oldest *lios* woman asked, 'Should we let him have it?' They shrieked in one voice, 'Yes, we should.' I could hardly contain my excitement," Fachtna continued. "They told me to walk on ahead, which I did until an oak tree blocked my way and there, embedded in it, was—"

"Cúchulainn's golden ball," Aisling interjected quickly.

"Yes, yes, yes," said Fachtna. "I stretched my hand toward it and felt a magnetic force draw me deep into the tree trunk which opened out before me. The oldest *lios* woman pushed me into an awaiting carriage which took off on tracks, just like the Luas, and whisked me away for miles on end, criss-crossing other tracks which I now know link the *sídhe* forts of Cruachan, Eamhain, Tara, Newgrange, and Ailleach. When it stopped, I was blindfolded, led to this room, handed a feather duster, shown a pile of gossamer cloths, and told that since I was so fond of golden balls, I could spend the rest of my days buffing them up, along with all the *sídhe* treasures. I was warned never to touch Cúchulainn's *sliotar* or my hands would rot."

"And?"

A little magpie flew in through one of the bronze latticed windows carrying in its claws ruby and sapphire earrings, and in its beak a bar of Cadbury's milk chocolate. Fachtna explained that this was the magpie's busiest season with the Wexford Opera Festival in full swing, hotel windows open and jewellery on display.

"Do you mean the brooch is stolen?" Aisling asked.

"Yes," answered Fachtna, explaining that one of his jobs was to record provenances, and that the magpie had already dropped off a matching ruby and sapphire necklace.

"What are provenances?"

"Histories of ownership," explained Fachtna. "Magpies love open windows which offer them irresistible opportunities for rich pickings."

The magpie dropped the earrings and chocolate into Fachtna's hand. He hungrily ate the chocolate and didn't even offer Aisling a square. The bird then flew out the window once more.

"Magpies are thieves," observed Aisling.

"Not by choice," said Fachtna.

In no time at all the magpie returned with a gold ring, not unlike a Claddagh one, in its beak, hovered over Aisling, dropped it onto her hand, and said: "If you need an update on anything down here, rub this ring with your index finger and it will relay instant live images to you."

"That's great! Thanks a million," she said slipping the ring onto her finger.

"What brings you here, by the way?" Fachtna asked.

"My grandmother went missing in 1965 and I think she may be down here somewhere," answered Aisling. "I want to bring her home to grandad."

"Promise to get me out too if you manage to escape this hell-hole."

"I promise."

"Friends?" he asked.

She looked down at the two hands clasped in friendship. "Friends," she replied.

The magpie took off.

"But," Fachtna looked over his shoulder before whispering, "I'll not leave without Cúchulainn's golden *sliotar*."

"Shhh," said Aisling. "The *sídhe* servant on watch duty is coming over."

Hardly were the words out of her mouth when hundreds of the *slua sídhe* swarmed into the gallery, led by a furious Maebh. Fachtna was lifted on high and taken out of sight. Aisling looked around the treasure *lios*. Even the *sídhe* servants had disappeared into thin air. She was all alone.

Chapter Seven

A Daring Theft
and a Hasty Exit

Oh my God! Were they coming back for her next? Aisling needed to move on quickly while the coast was clear. The *slua sídhe* were clearly furious at Fachtna's plans to leave the *lios*, taking with him their precious *sliotar*. Aisling rubbed the magpie's ring with her index finger and, as promised, it showed her pictures. Fachtna sat on a bench alongside others in a dingy dungeon cell under a large sign which read, "We have ways of making you talk". Towering over him on her witch's stool, one of the *sídhe* threatened to cudgel him senseless.

Something light brushed against her shoulder. The little magpie flew across the room and dropped a gold chain, which it said needed minor repair, on an elm table.

"I never realized you magpies are so busy," she said.

"That's our *geasa* for you," it replied.

"Your *geasa*, what's that?"

"It's being honour-bound to do something, even when it's against your will."

"So, you made a vow?"

"Not quite," the magpie replied. "A vow is made voluntarily but a *geasa* is imposed."

"Who put you under the *geasa*?"

"Oonagh did, a long time ago, in Fionn Mac Cumhaill's time."

"I'd love to hear all about it but I'd better get going or Maebh and her mob might snatch me and bring me to the dungeon," said Aisling.

"They'll take their time with the interrogation."

"Will Fachtna be all right?"

"Let's hope so," said the magpie, sitting on the velvet couch beside her and folding its wings. It began: "It was winter long ago in Doire 'n Chairn. A carpet of snow covered the forest floor. I was on my way to the concert."

"What concert?"

"The blackbird of Doire 'n Chairn's concert. It's very well known. I took a shortcut across the Fianna's shooting range, foolishly forgetting they were in training. I was dazed by a stone flung from Oscar's catapult, lost height and slumped to the ground, fast losing consciousness. A nightingale let out a plaintive wail. I was just giving up the ghost when the emergency *sídhe* ambulance corps arrived, administered first aid, and then flew me to their base at Dún Gréine. Oonagh instructed the medics to place me on a mushroom-shaped copper stool and sent for Darach the herbalist, who brought his

Gladstone bag of comfrey, rosemary, purple foxgloves, and other fresh herbs. These were beaten to a pulp with a mortar and pestle, rendered to a juice, poured into a half walnut shell and put to my beak. Drop by drop the potion trickled down my gullet. Then I was brought to Doctor Cnámh Sídhe's special care unit where I soon recovered. I had an unexpected visitor one day."

"Queen Dracula?"

"Yes," said the magpie. "She bared her blood-dripping fangs and snarled that I owed her big time."

"What did the she-devil want?"

"Gold, silver, diamonds, rubies, sapphires—you name it, she craved it. She put all us magpies under the *geasa*."

"So that's why the gallery is jam-packed with precious stuff," remarked Aisling.

"The *sídhe* recycle everything—their jewellers, goldsmiths, and silversmiths turn ugly pieces into outstanding works of art, like the true Tara Brooch."

"I'll add that to my notes later," said Aisling. "Can the *geasa* be broken?" she asked, touched by the magpie's plight.

"Yes, when blackbirds sing once more in Doire 'n Chairn. By the way, Aisling, have you seen the true Tara Brooch?"

"Yes, it's fab! I saw it in the National Museum."

"That's only a replica, made in our workshop in the early Christian period, and found by a child on Bettystown beach in 1850. The Vikings probably dropped it as they headed home with their loot. The true Tara Brooch and all precious original objects are kept here where they belong. The old hag of Tara, who guarded it night and day, used the Tara Brooch, which shows the movement of planet earth from one age to another, as a Zodiacal calendar."

"It's hard to get my head around all this," Aisling commented.

"When the old hag of Tara saw me leave her fort with the precious brooch dangling from my beak she shrieked and called her demons to chase me."

"Demons?"

"You'll pardon my saying so, but you know very little of our rich heritage," said the magpie, who was getting frustrated with all the interruptions. "The demons inhabit the air."

"They do?"

"Yes. They and the old hag set off like the hammers of Hell and chased me westwards. I had no option but to keep going over the Atlantic Ocean. I thought the old hag would give up the chase, but no such luck. She cut a twig from a gorse bush on Aran, struck it with her magic wand and changed it into a sailing *currach*, hopped on board, and she and the demons sailed across the Atlantic in hot pursuit of me."

"Scary!"

"My feathers stood on end like the quills of a hedgehog."

"Grandad says it's a steep and thorny path to heaven."

"What's that got to do with anything?" The magpie, tiring of Aisling's interruptions, drummed impatiently with its foot on the arm of the velvet couch before continuing: "The *slua sídhe* of the air, noticing my predicament, flew to my assistance. The old hag never misses a trick, so she struck the demons with her wand and changed them into hawks which chased me, their pointed talons poised and ready to tear me apart. Fortunately, the *slua sídhe* hid me in a storm cloud and we flew all the way

The Children of Lir. (28, 2011)

back to Lake Dearravaragh. There they changed themselves into swans and sheltered me under their wings."

"Just like Fionnuala sheltered Conn, Aodh, and Fiachra on the sea of Moyle," said Aisling, who knew the story of the Children of Lir almost by heart.

"Don't deviate," the magpie said crossly, "it's very distracting. The old hag changed the demons into stoats and weasels and they attacked the swans which were affording me my bodyguard. Fortunately, the underwater *sídhe* sent up a giant wave and almost drowned the old hag and her rat-pack.

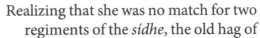

Realizing that she was no match for two regiments of the *sídhe*, the old hag of Tara gave up the chase and headed home, whereupon the *slua sídhe* hoisted me up onto the back of the wind and flew me to Dún Gréine where I slid down the rainbow into the earth with the Tara Brooch intact."

"Great story!"

"I must away," said the magpie as it flew out the open latticed window.

"Wait a minute," said Aisling. "Have you by any chance seen my grandmother, Bláithín, on your travels?"

But the magpie had already flown out the latticed window.

Aisling wondered if Miss Moore would believe that the true Tara Brooch was in the underworld. She would probably pass some cutting remark like, "It's obvious to all that you've been away with the fairies again." Maybe, if she brought back Cúchulainn's *sliotar* her teacher would have a change of heart. What a brainwave! Aisling stood on an oak stool, reached up with her blackthorn stick, poked at Cúchulainn's golden ball, which toppled out of the silver mesh into her gossamer cloth. How was she going to smuggle it out? Another brainwave! With her Ariadne thread and little needle, she sewed it into the hem of her skirt then tapped it with her blackthorn stick, believing that it would become invisible, but it didn't oblige, so she gave a harder tap. Success! It vanished. Great stuff! Now all she needed was a way out.

The stars, planets and eighty-eight constellations were sparkling underfoot. If the code was correct and she stepped on the moon it should bring her to a new zone.

Chapter Eight

Dead or Alive?
Surprise! Surprise!

The moon unlocked a hidden trap door which must have opened and shut ever so quickly. A puzzled Aisling scratched her head as she figured out that she had fallen through and landed on a staircase. God only knew where it led, but at least, for now, she was out of Maebh's clutches. Who was that white-bearded man at the bottom of the stairs? He reminded her of Santa Claus. Was it Christmas time here? Would she get pressies? The thought of Christmas made her homesick. Jackie and Seán, her mum and dad, must be distraught by now. Had they cut short their Mediterranean cruise to look for her? Were search parties out night and day? Had she been declared missing, presumed dead, like Bláithín was in 1965?

She wished she could reassure everyone that she was all right but, even if she had the choice, there was no turning back. She was on a mission just like the explorers of old. She couldn't take her eyes off the solemn faced, bearded man, who was dressed in yellow and green striped trousers tucked into grey bootees.

"Excuse me sir," she called ever so politely, "could you tell me where I am?"

He put down his long-stemmed dúidín and book before joining his hands as if in prayer.

"*Sanctóir*," he whispered, putting his index finger to his lips, "*sanctóir*."

"*Sanctóir*?"

"Sacred space," he replied in a whisper.

"Are you the underworld Santa Claus?"

"Not I."

"Is there a dungeon here? I'm looking for my friend, Fachtna. Maebh and her *slua* put him in a cell somewhere. She has

54

whips and handcuffs and other stuff. My grandmother is missing too since 1965. She may need my help too. Tell me if I'm intruding."

"You ask too many questions, child."

"Should I call my underworld guide, No-Name."

"Do not. No-Name is most unwelcome in my *sanctóir*."

"Are you the druid I saw outside a cave a few days ago? No-Name said you're a *saoi*, and that you guys know all about the future. Could you help me see mine?"

"Answer to request is negative."

"What's your name?"

"Cian."

He bowed his head and walked down the passage. Aisling followed, zipping her lips together in an effort not to chatter. She was intrigued by some padlocked heavy brass-beaded oak trunks in the corridor. Curiosity got the better of her.

"What's in the trunks?" she asked.

"Genealogies."

"Can I see them?"

"Answer negative. Druid children study them."

"Do druid children have to go to school?"

"Answer positive."

"This underworld is one big educational establishment, as far as I can see." Aisling said with a frown.

"Astronomy, genealogy, music, mathematics, ancient laws, and the Táin, a famous story engraved in the night sky are memorized by all druids who, like Amergin, astronomer and poet of the Milesians, know wherein the sun sets, the ages of the moon, and that no land surpasses this island of the setting sun," replied Cian.

"Whose ashes are in the urns on the window ledges?"

"Death, my child, is non-existent here. The urns contain seeds of wisdom and knowledge," he answered, walking on ahead.

Aisling dallied behind and, shifting nervously from foot to foot, furtively sneaked a handful of seeds from the nearest urn and popped them into her pocket, tapping them with the blackthorn stick. She hurried after Cian who had entered into a round room which was not unlike the treasure *lios*. There she noticed five austere, lifelike stone statues.

"Your ancestors," said Cian. "You are most fortunate to meet them."

She got a fit of the giggles. "Sure they're dead as dodos," she said. "If you're pulling my leg, it's not funny."

"Offer them your hand in friendship," he commanded, ignoring her laughter.

"No prob," said Aisling wrinkling her nose in disdain as she crossed the room and touched the hand of the lady statue. Instantly she froze in shock. The hand was human flesh and bone. She ran behind Cian for shelter.

"I thought you were joking," she protested.

"I jest not. Show some respect. We have recorded, both in drawings and in Ogham, everything about your most ancient ancestors in our *Book of Invasions*. It is on view in our library. When your people accept that we are as real as they are, we shall welcome them here to view the treasures of the *sídhe*."

"*Sídhe* tours! They'll be booked up in no time."

"Meet Caesair, Noah's granddaughter. She is the first woman to have set foot on this fair land."

Aisling giggled again. "I suppose Noah will appear next with all the animals."

"Sneering becomes you not. Forty days before the Flood, Caesair sailed here out of the Grecian mist with fifty maidens and three brave men—Fintan, Ladhra, and Bith. They settled on Sliabh Bheatha."

"Am I to believe there were seventeen women to each man? That's a record." Aisling was top of the class in mental arithmetic.

"You have much to learn, Aisling. The underworld library charts not alone their arrival, but also that of all the early invasions and the exact position of the stars and planets at the time of their arrival. Our scribes are presently recording the arrival for holidays of Charon, who is taking a break from ferrying souls across the Styx, and Zeus and Apollo from Mount Olympus, who holiday here each year. Our children are well versed in their history. Would you like to see the charts?"

"Yeah, I would, but I have to find my friend, Fachtna, and my grandmother, Bláithín, first. Any chance you've seen either of them?" she asked. Caesair hesitated a moment and then shook her head.

"And you are?" Aisling asked, moving on to the next statue.

"Parthalon. I came and settled here with my people when Abraham was twenty years old."

"Hope you're no friend of Abraham's," Aisling said, "How gross to threaten to burn his son Isaac."

"I am a contemporary of his," said Parthalon.

"Mad! No-one will believe me when I tell them I was talking with a contemporary of Abraham."

"I've been around for a long time."

"Any chance you remember seeing my grandmother, Bláithín, about 50 years ago?"

"No, but maybe Neimhí here, whose people built the forts of Tara, Cruachan, and Eamhain has some information on her. Access to the underworld, as you know, is via the Nemesian-built forts. Have you met Aisling's grandmother, Bláithín, Neimhí?" he asked of the next statue which was turning to flesh and blood. To Aisling's disappointment, Neimhí shook his head.

"Maybe Sláinge of the Fir Bolg's, or Nuadhat noticed her," he suggested.

"They're here too? Those Fir Bolgs were hairy hulks," she said suppressing a giggle.

"Yes," answered Neimhí. "We five were the first of the early settlers in this country. We are immortal. Death, as you know it, only came with the Milesians."

"Miss Moore told our class all about you," Aisling said. "I'd love to have my photo taken with you all."

They laughed.

"Sorry, we can't oblige," said Nuadhat, "but you may shake my hand and make a wish."

He offered his silver hand to her. Aisling shut her eyes as she shook it and made a wish that she would find Fachtna and her grandmother and return safely home.

"It's time to enter the inner *sanctóir*," said Cian, "you will join us, Aisling."

"Thank you, thank you all," said Aisling, who could scarcely credit that she had met her earliest ancestors who could trace their roots back to the dawn of time. Parthalon, Neimhí, Sláinge, and Nuadhat followed Cian into the inner *sanctóir*. Caesair gave Aisling a nudge. "I know something which might help you," she whispered, "we'll talk later."

Chapter Nine

One step forwards,
two steps back

Streams of water gushed out from the *sanctóir* walls. "The waters of life," Cian explained, "which separate the outer and inner *sanctóir*." The waters parted in front of them, just as the Red Sea had done for Moses long ago. Aisling clung to Nuadhat's silver hand and felt safe.

A tall oak tree loomed ahead and beside it was a stone chair, set in a small, star-burst, crop circle design.

"Wait here," said Cian, as he and the ancients went on ahead. Aisling saw before her a triangle of nine standing stones grouped in threes around a dolmen-like altar.

In the distance, a stooped figure plucked roots and plants from the earth, placed them in a bronze cauldron and muttered incantations over them. Feidhlim, druidess and earth's guardian, wove her way in and around the standing stones, then came forward and scattered a handful of earth from the cauldron on Aisling's shoes. Some ante-diluvian ritual, Aisling reckoned. She knew the word because her mum often used it to describe her dad's family. Druids, wearing speckled bull hides, emerged chanting from one of the passageways. They seemed to float on air and reminded Aisling of the Hare Krishnas who regularly chanted in Grafton Street.

"I am Cathbad," the chief druid said. "Tell your people to listen to and play the sacred life-giving music which rises from the bowels of the earth, as blind Carolan did." Cathbad handed Cian a golden sickle and sat down with his minstrels in front of the standing stones nearest Aisling. A second group of druids, dressed in dull grey tunics, carrying parchment scrolls and chanting genealogies, entered the sanctuary.

"I am Glún. I represent our bardic schools," the oldest one said. "Tell your people to preserve our stories and sagas for future generations." He handed Cian a bronze breastplate and sat down with his bards. The third passageway was now thronged with druids wreathed from head to toe in oak leaves.

"I am the astronomer Grian," said their leader to Aisling. "On the longest day of the year, the sun rises directly over Cloch Fáil, the tallest of these standing stones, penetrates earth and energizes our sacred ground. Tell your people to return to the study of the stars and planets."

He handed Cian a small, round disc.

Cathbad's druids took up lyre, harp and cymbals and played a tune. Down one of the passageways, dressed in white robes, ran little druidic children, led by Oisín, Tom Tom, Sadhbh Louise and Aaron, chanting a nursery rhyme.

> *Muc ogham*
> *Cearc ogham*
> *Ogham uisce*
> *Cos ogham*
> *Srón ogham*
> *Tusa is mise.*
>
> *Muc ogham*
> *Cearc ogham*
> *Ogham usice*
> *Cos ogham*
> *Srón ogham*
> *Tusa is mise.*

The children too sat down in front of the dolmen altar. Cian went to where Aisling waited at the oak tree and handed her the golden sickle.

"Cut a single branch of mistletoe from this tree," he said most solemnly.

Aisling did as bidden.

"Place it here on this bronze breastplate," he said, "and petition survival and safe passage through the underworld."

Aisling did so.

He then took the round disc and placed it in the centre of her brow where it held fast. "Our third eye brings you perception beyond ordinary sight," he said, "for the duration of your travels here below."

"Come, worship with us," he said, walking towards the altar.

Aisling, overwhelmed with joy at being accepted into their midst, knelt with Cian, Feidhlim, the druids and her ancestors in prayer. The druids began to chant:

> *Thank ye gods for all ye share:*
> *Earth and water; fire and air;*
> *Almighty ones, spirit breathe*
> *On us, your children here, this eve.*
>
> *Mountain, valley, sky and sea*
> *Hear us chant in harmony.*
> *Wind, rain and morning dew*
> *In us, your children, life renew.*

The chants, which were to continue until sunrise and were to end with a ceremonial walk around the ancient fort of Tara, were rudely interrupted by the arrival of a shrieking No-Name, accompanied by hordes of hyperactive look-alikes, who

shouted Aisling's name at the tops of their voices as they burst in on the sacred ceremony.

All within the temple froze. The little druids looked aghast. Cian let out a wail, as did Feidhlim and all the druids. He strode over to No-Name and his look-alikes, his ash wand raised high. Aisling heard their shrieks of terror. Cian returned, the ash wand still aloft, pointed it at Aisling and shook it angrily in her face. No-Name's cap zoomed off her head. The third eye was plucked from her brow. She was hauled backwards, flung on top of the huge stone seat which was set in the star-burst formation along with No-Name and friends. The stone seat groaned under their weight and started to burrow into the bowels of the earth, its strange cargo shocked into an eerie silence. Down, down, down into everlasting darkness, it Kango-hammered its way even further than she imagined possible into the depths of the underworld.

Aisling could cheerfully have wrung No-Name's neck. Why had he burst in on the druid's worship? She had been doing fine on her own. Had Fionnbharr, Oonagh, and Maebh put him up to this? Was it always going to be like this—one step forward and two steps back? No-Name must have known it was a sacrilege to interrupt druidic chants. Was it a deliberate ploy on his part to shame and embarrass her? Grandad Aonghus was right when he told her she was no match for *bobaireacht na sídhe*. She tightened her hold on the blackthorn stick. No-one was getting that. She wasn't defeated yet. She called No-Name. Silence! He didn't have to answer her now, did he? He was a free agent.

Plonk! The stone seat ground to a halt and bedded down. All was black, pitch black. No glittering diamonds or precious stones giving out their light down here. Only the glimmer of ruby-eyed lizards and wriggling glow-worms cast some light around. Once accustomed to the dark, Aisling became aware that she was in an enormous stone dungeon. A trickle of light filtered slowly around it revealing rows of stone seats above a stone arena. Sullen, grim-faced creatures stared down at her. Grotesque, red-nosed *sídhe*, thin lips pursed together, facial expressions as stony as the seats they sat on, glared at her in a belligerent hostile manner.

The bushy-bearded No-Namers, their spiky red hair sticking out in all directions, pushed her roughly aside, tumbled out of the stone chair, ran up the steps and joined the restless *Clurichái n* who were dressed in pale blue stockings, short brown boots, brown leather aprons and red caps, and were hopping in and out of their seats, turning giant somersaults, leap-frogging over one another, pulling the lizards' legs, pinching the glittering toads, wriggling like glow-worms, and chattering at speed in strange, high-pitched voices. Bald-headed, dwarf-like *sídhe*, smoking clay *dúidíní*, peaked ears covering each side of their heads, stood sullenly in the aisles, scowling at Aisling.

Seated in the front rows, dressed in red from head to toe, were the capricious *fir* and *mná dearga*. These were the mischievous little *sídhe* men and women dressed in red from head to toe. Out of nowhere a tiny lobster pot appeared on the floor. "Hope they are not going to use me as bait! Ridiculous thought!" Aisling scolded herself, knowing that there was no way on earth she could fit into the lobster pot which was about the size of a *sliotar*. But she wasn't *on earth*, was she? A *fear dearg* approached, picked her up with one hand, blew on her and carried her across the stone floor. To her horror, she began to shrink in size until she was no bigger than a Barbie doll. She screamed as she was popped through the tiny door of the lobster pot. She called out for No-Name but, in the sea of *sídhe* faces, it was impossible to identify him. Click! The door closed.

"Hurray! Hurray!" shouted the little causeway people. The *fear dearg* struck the ground three times with his right foot. The lobster pot, with its terrified Aisling, began to rock and roll, all the while growing a hard leather shell. She could just about see the sea of sneering faces through two tiny peepholes.

"Hurling!" shouted No-Name. She recognized his voice.

"Hurling," echoed all the *sídhe* in great glee. "Hurling."

"*Clurichái n* against the *Dearga*," shouted No-Name.

"*Clurichán* against the *Dearga*," echoed all the *sídhe.* "*Clurichán* against the *Dearga.*"

Through the peepholes, Aisling saw fifteen *Dearga* discard their cloaks and come onto the pitch. Fifteen *Clurichán* took of their leather aprons and lined up opposite them. The referee appeared. A *sídhe* woman, dressed in ivy-leaf cap, dress of spider's web, shoes of butterfly wings and cloak of thistledown, ran onto the pitch blowing a blade of grass. She shouted at the top of her voice, "*Ar aghaidh libh! Ar aghaidh libh!*" The match began.

Aisling squinted her eyes and peered through the peepholes at the hurley sticks which looked alive and ready for battle. She remembered with panic Fionnbharr telling her that hurleys were used as weapons long ago while Oonagh smirked at her.

"Ouch!" A fierce blow struck the right side of her face and she was pucked up and down the stone causeway to thunderous cheers, sneers and applause. She buried her throbbing head in her hands and sobbed. Wham, bang, clash, smash, biff, bash! The *Dearga* played with the wind and were in flying form. They dribbled, jostled, tackled, and roared obscenities at the hottempered *Clurichán* who took schelps out of their legs before scoring an almighty goal from seventeen yards out. The maddened *Dearga* retaliated with two hat-tricks and the pitch bore a trail of scorch marks as the players belted the *sliotar* faster than the speed of light from one end of the causeway to the other. The *Clurichán* goalie executed a magnificent save just before half-time when the little referee raised her blade of grass to her lips and blew.

A bevy of cheerleaders, dressed in pink satin mini-skirts and purple waist-coats swarmed onto the pitch, lifted the *Clurichán* onto their shoulders to the delight of the cheering crowds. A second throng of cheerleaders, dressed in silver mini-dresses and gold capes, smothered the *Dearga* with kisses, and their supporters almost lifted the corbelled roof from the stone causeway with their cheers. *Sídhe* waiters served the thirsty teams goblets of ivy and dandelion juices and the *sídhe* marching band, also known as the biggest little band in the underworld, dressed in their distinctive blue and scarlet uniforms, played their old favourite, "*Ó Sliotar Amú*", on silver drums, golden trumpets, clashing cymbals, and obnoxious-sounding brass horns which struck terror into Aisling with every note.

The players then took up their positions for the second half. Wham, bang, clash of the ash, bash, smash, lash of the leather! The *sliotar* was pucked up and down as this half was contested even more furiously than the first. The bloodthirsty *Clurichán*, using their hurls like battle axes, almost beheaded the gutsy fullback of the *Dearga*. "Foul," screeched the ref and awarded a penalty. The *Dearga* took full advantage of it, scoring a dramatic goal. The enraged *Clurichán* struck back inflicting a plethora of savage ocular injuries on them. Casualties were removed on stretchers as the match moved into injury time.

The captain of the *Dearga*, sniffing victory, slash-hooked the *Clurichán* centre-back and almost severed his jawbone. Medics sprang to attention and sprayed it. A penalty was awarded. The jaw-drooping *Clurichán* gritted his teeth, took up position and scored. The ref blew her blade of grass. The match was over. The *fear dearg* struck the floor three times with his foot. The leather shell disintegrated and fell away. A white-faced Aisling, shaking like a leaf, wondered what might happen next.

Chapter Ten

Crop circles,
human cloning, and
underworld gangsters

ot for long. The *fear dearg* swooped down, opened the
door of the *sliotar* cage, scooped Aisling out, raised her
on high to the jeers of all in the stone causeway, carried her
over to a low, moss-covered stone wishing well, sat her down,
blew her back to size and sneered, "Your every wish shall *not*
be granted."

"Your every wish shall *not* be granted," mocked the *sídhe*,
"Your every wish shall *not* be granted."

Aisling lowered her gaze to avoid their contemptuous
glances, and noticed what resembled the number four incised
on the cobbled floor. She planted her feet on it. A whirlwind of
grey dust whooshed past her, almost knocking her off the wall,
sped clockwise around the well and then settled. The *fir dearga*
and night riders had returned from their nightly adventures.
Rushes sprang up nearby as they dismounted. They sat on
high-backed *súgán* chairs in front of their audience who were
looking forward to entertaining tales of their escapades in the
upperworld. These night riders were Giob, Geab, Srón,
Sleamhain, Cogar, and Mogar. The *Cluricháin*, usually as restless as monkeys, were quiet as mice. The shimmering toads,
ruby-eyed lizards, and glittering glow-worms toned down their

lights. The bald-headed dwarves smoking their *dúidíní*, cocked their ears.

Giob opened the proceedings.

"We rode out the causeway door as usual at the bewitching hour. The east wind took us west and the west wind took us east." Aisling pricked up her ears. "As we passed over the cornfields of Eamhain some ears of corn spilled out of our bag of tricks, grew heads and bodies, sprouted arms and legs, and danced sixteen-hand reels in O'Flaherty's cornfield, etching wondrous designs with every step."

"So that explains the mysterious crop circles," thought Aisling, "very interesting indeed."

Geab continued; "We were riding past sculptor Ó Hógáin's workshop. He does his best work between midnight and dawn. Ó Hógáin was putting some finishing touches to a giant stag. We hopped through the window, popped a pinhead of salted butter into the stag's mouth whereupon it sprang to life, scooped Ó Hógáin onto its back and rode out under Orion's Belt across hedges and ditches, its rider yelling blue murder. It leapt across the Cliffs of Moher and galloped straight back to the studio as the salted butter evaporated and off-loaded a dazed Ó Hógáin, who is still scratching his head and puzzling over whether or not to give up his trade altogether."

The *sídhe* folk were rocking with laughter in the aisles. Srón and Sleamhain were fidgeting in their seats, dying to regale the audience with their night's escapades. These two were as slippery as eels and could sniff trouble a mile away.

"We rode like the hammers of Hell out through the trap door at the midnight hour," said Srón. "The lamp posts were flying by like the teeth of a comb."

"Joy riders!" said the *fear dearg*, beaming at them.

"We galloped into the court-yard of Goat's Castle on Thorn Island where the Living History Society's performance of the Mediaeval Drama, "Plops, Slops, and Chamber Pots," was in full swing. The Lady of the Manor in period gown, without as much as a *garde l'eau*, threw caution and a bucket of slops to the wind drenching our gorgeous black capes."

Sleamhain took up the story. "She got instant comeuppance. A few *sídhe* darts aimed at the offending bucket and it whisked up into the air, back-flipped and rammed itself upside-down on her shoulders where it held fast. Some wise guy suggested buying no-frills Ryanair flights and heading to Ascott for Ladies Day's Most Sensational Model and Hat competition. Dún Laoghaire and Rathdown fire brigade, in response to a 999 call from a member of the audience, arrived but failed to prise it off."

The causeway audience squealed with glee. They knew that no power on earth could trump *sidhe* hocus pocus.

Cogar and Mogar were next to recount their night's shenanigans. The trap-door swung open. A beautiful girl, bewildered and forlorn, was ushered in.

"Síle na gCláirseach," sniggered Cogar.

"We were spellbound by this vision of beauty at Tara's Mound of the Hostages and enchanted by the haunting Bunting airs delicately performed on her wire-strung harp. Mogar here waved a wisp of straw over her which lulled her into a deep sleep, found an old log, prayed the cloning *ortha* over it so that it took on her shape and form. We lifted Sile onto his mare and rode here to the causeway."

Mogar then addressed Aisling: "Would you like us to clone your *spitting* image from a lump of wood? We could drop it off at your grandad's house and they could call off the search-party."

Aisling shook her head vigorously.

"Are you sure?" Mogar asked before continuing, "The real Síle na gCláirseach will never be missed by her own people, as the clone at home is the *splitting* image of her."

All in the causeway squealed with glee.

"You must have heard of Dolly the sheep," Cogar continued. "Eavesdropping scientists from the Roslin Institute in Edinburgh holidaying in these parts over-heard, memorized and used our *ortha*, so you could say that Dolly's cloning was entirely due to us. Your people put her down with a lethal injection when she was only six years of age. What do you think of that?"

All in the causeway squealed with glee and applauded. Aisling wrinkled her nose in disgust and shuddered. The *fear dearg* bowed low before Síle. "Welcome to our world," he said with a Jekyll and Hyde smile

"Welcome to our world," echoed all the *sídhe*, "welcome to our world."

The scene reminded Aisling of Fionnbharr and Oonagh's banquet. She wondered what treachery was in store for Síle who was being led from the trap door down the stone steps by a horde of No-Namers to the *fear dearg* who ordered, "Bring the *deoch dearmaid*." Oh no! Once Síle sipped that drink she would very soon forget all about her own people and become more like the *sídhe* than the *sídhe* themselves and swell the numbers of the disappeared without trace list back home in Ireland. There was a hushed silence. A waiter arrived with a golden goblet on a silver tray. Aisling stared in disbelief.

Yes! It was No-Name. He stood on a stool, offered the goblet to a mesmerized Síle who raised it to her lips. He deftly tipped the contents into her mouth and bowed to the audience who cheered as the *fear dearg* gave the thumbs-up sign. Síle was then taken behind a screen by the *sídhe* wardrobe mistress and emerged wearing red shoes and stockings, a red gown and a veil. The causeway erupted with applause. The *sídhe* folk hopped, bopped, turned head over heels, and did triple somersaults up and down the aisles. The *fear dearg* took Síle's hand in his, walked through a guard of honour formed by the lizards, caterpillars and glow-worms, as garlands of primroses and four-leaved clover were thrown at them. "*Sliocht sleacht ar shliocht bhur sleachta*," shouted the *sídhe*, "*sliocht sleacht ar shliocht bhur sleachta*."

No-Name brought a golden urn containing wedding ointment with which he marked their foreheads, a small needle with which he pierced both their wrists, and a tiny topaz thimble into which he drained their blood. The wedding festivities then started. Aisling fingered the friendship ring and, as the magpie had promised, it relayed pictures to her. Fachtna came into perspective, sitting in his cell looking very dejected. She was now determined to escape with him and re-introduce grandad Aonghus to Senan, his boyhood friend. The scene changed. She viewed with astonishment a *sídhe* army buzzing around the treasure *lios*, peering behind the velvet couches and under the marble chess tables. They looked fit to burst as they roused the servants from their siestas and pointed in disbelief at the empty silver mesh on the ceiling.

Next she viewed the entrance to the druid's grove where No-Name's cap hung from a mistletoe branch on the oak tree. Oisín, Tom Tom, Sadhbh Louise, and Aaron proudly stood nearby on guard duty. Back in the treasure *lios*, the little magpie flew in through the window, another treasure dangling from its beak. Oh no! It couldn't possibly be grandad Aonghus' gold fob watch and chain, a family heirloom. But it was. Aisling recognized the enamel face and resolved to get it back.

The scene flashed to the druids' grove. It was sunrise and the sun's intense red and orange rays struck the *Cloch Fáil* and cut through the earth. Aisling was bathed in its warm glow as it struck the mossy stone wall of the wishing well where she sat, her feet resting on the cobbled floor. A magnetic force travelled through her, propelled her upwards as if from a launching pad, shot her through the open trap door in the causeway roof to where all was extraordinarily bright.

She had entered a new and even stranger world.

Chapter Eleven

Three into one does go

Aisling was thrilled to have escaped the low-life in the stone causeway. Fortunately for her, she was standing on the Jupiter symbol incised on the cobbled floor in the stone causeway which was activated when the sun's rays struck the *Cloch Fáil* and penetrated through to the wishing well. Had it happened by design or by chance? If the former: full marks to ingenuity of the *sídhe*. If the latter: maybe Lady Luck was with her at last. The magnetic force in her weakened and she landed with a gentle bump in a lush valley in front of a giant iron-wheel, its rainbow-coloured spokes whirring round and round. Three men in one were spinning it. Weird or what?

"Goibniú," the iron god introduced himself, swung to the right and introduced Creidne, the metal god, and to the left, Luchtaine, the wheel god. "We three gods of Art hand-forge and repair all the weapons of the Tuatha Dé Danann and have done so since the dawn of time," Goibniú proudly announced. "Do you wish to place an order?"

"No, not exactly," said Aisling, "I just escaped the stone causeway and I'm looking for a safe haven. Everyone here hates my guts, No-Name, the *Fear Dearg*, Fionnbharr, Oonagh, Maebh, Cian, and the druids. It's a strange new world here."

"Are you a crusading modern day Columbus?" asked the iron god with a chuckle.

"Yes," retorted Aisling, who knew a little European history, "and Queen Isabella sponsored my trip."

"Fortunately for you, Jupiter's red spot was activated at sunrise. Had you placed your feet on one of its sixty-three moons, you would still be in orbit," said the metal god.

"Can I come in?" Aisling repeated, "please."

"We'll have to put our heads together on that one," said the wheel god, winking at his other parts. "We will talk about it on our break. We don't encourage outsiders to our secret world," he added before he and the metal god split away.

"Neither do the Freemasons." Aisling's dad Seán, a bibliophile, had a collection of books on Freemasonry which she was forbidden to read as they were top secret.

"We are masons in the oldest tradition," he answered. "We offer our services free for the benefit of the universe."

"Services?"

"Yes, with our fertility wheel we constantly spin new energies into the earth. We have done so for thousands of years. Should this wheel stop spinning, even for a fraction of a second as you know it, life would end, rivers, streams and wells become polluted, the air you breathe stagnate, your crops decay, and your animals and people die. We spin fertility and hold back the tides of destruction and disease."

"I'll record that in my notebook."

The wheel god and the metal god returned, fused with the iron god and together the three-in-one and one-in-three spun the wheel faster and faster. Aisling was trying to figure out a way to get to the other side of the wheel, which had huge pillars on either side, when an auburn-haired goddess wearing an emerald green cloak over a crimson gown approached. A bluebird chirped on each shoulder.

"The goddess Eadaoin, our janitor, has come to invite you in," the iron god informed her.

"On condition you spin the wheel of life for a while," the goddess said, adding, "everyone lends a hand here."

"No problem," said Aisling, putting her hand to the wheel and giving it a push. Then, horror of horrors! The three-in-one gods removed their hands from it and joined Eadaoin. Aisling was all alone, pushing with all her might. The wheel was a dead weight. But, there was no turning back. The future of the universe was in her hands. The world as we know it could be annihilated in a split second if she stopped spinning. Heart pounding, legs wobbling, beads of sweat dripping to the ground, arms worn to a frazzle, she realized to her horror that she was losing her grip on the fertility wheel.

One of Eadaoin's bluebirds winged its way to Aisling and dropped some blackberries into her mouth. Revitalized, she spun the wheel with great gusto, but not for long. It slowed down and ground almost to a halt. She let out a blood-curdling scream of despair as her strength ebbed. Strong arms lifted her away. Charon, an old, grey-haired boatman from the Styx who was holidaying in Brugh na Bóinne, took her in his arms and laid her down.

"Lucky for you I'm here on my annual visit," he said. "Ferrying poor souls to the other side is second nature to me. You were at death's door when I heard your cry of despair. There's no toll charge," he added with a wry smile. "The Daghda wants to meet you."

"Who's the Daghda?"

"Father god of the Tuatha Dé Danann and my oldest friend," he answered. "He brought his people here to safety after the Battles of Tailteann and Mis. Manannán, the sea god, gave them all the gift of invisibility."

"I wish I had the gift of invisibility," said Aisling. "Do you like it here?"

"Yes. Greek gods and goddesses have been coming here since the dawn of time. Zeus and Apollo are over there talking with Aonghus Óg and Caer. Apollo and Aonghus Óg are boyhood friends, you know."

"How come?" asked Aisling.

"Caesair sailed to this ancient isle out of our Grecian mists forty days before the Flood, and Parthalon and the Tuatha Dé Danann followed. We are welcome here in Brugh na Bóinne just as the Daghda, Eadaoin, Aonghus Óg, Brigid, and all the others are welcome on our Mount Olympus.

"You are most welcome to visit us sometime in the future," he added. "Now rest a while and Eadaoin will bring you to meet the Daghda."

Aisling shut her eyes and fell asleep.

Chapter Twelve

In every gain there's loss, In every loss there's gain

She dreamed of a beautiful nymph named Daphne running through the woods, pursued by a young Apollo who loved her dearly. Her strength began to fail. "Help me father," she cried, "I do not want a lover." Her father Peneus, the river god, who loved her more than life, heard her plea and made her limbs grow stiff. Tree bark grew around her, her arms became branches; her feet rooted in the earth and her beautiful face became a tree top. Apollo wrapped his arms around it. "You shall be my tree always," he said. "I shall wear you woven as a wreath in my crown and display you on my harp and your leaves will always be fresh and green." Daphne bowed her laurel head in gratitude.

The goddess Eadaoin nudged Aisling out of her sleep. "The Daghda wears a sprig of laurel on the harp given him by Apollo," she said.

"How do you know I was dreaming of Apollo?" she asked.

"We are your dream-weavers," she replied, "and Apollo, Zeus and old Charon who rescued you, are the Daghda's guests of honour at our evening meal tonight. Come, the Daghda awaits you."

They walked through flowers, past a sleeping serpent coiled around an oak tree. It looked so gentle, Aisling stroked it. Dragons, cockerels, wolves and wild boars walked about freely.

"Tell me about the Daghda's harp," Aisling asked.

"The Fomorians stole it and hung it on the wall of a castle in which they were spending the night. The Daghda followed hard on their tracks. He and his gods burst through the door of the banqueting room before the Fomorians could grasp their weapons. The Daghda shouted, 'Harp, come to me' and it leapt from the wall into his arms. He played a *goltraí* and the Fomorians wept bitterly. This was followed by a *geantraí* which had them all laughing helplessly. Finally, the Daghda played a *suantraí* and they all nodded off to sleep. The Daghda and his gods brought his harp home to safety."

They had by now arrived at a clearing in the forest where the Daghda, Boann—chief goddess of Brugh na Bóinne, Apollo, Aonghus Óg, Caer, Charon, and Zeus were sitting on deerskins around a gurgling cauldron. The Daghda, ancient and grey-headed, wore a short brown tunic and horse hide boots with the hairy side out. He stood up as Aisling approached, offered her his club, and said: "Stir the cauldron for me and make sure you use the correct end or the food will perish."

Oh no, she thought, *not another test.* One of Eadaoin's birds flew down and perched on the tip of the club. Aisling plunged the other end into the cauldron and stirred. The Daghda chuckled as did all his guests. Aisling was happy to have passed another test in this strange world.

"The menu tonight," the Daghda announced, "is as follows:

Oysters from the bedrock of the river Corrib
Pale breast of Corcomroe goose
Floury Gort na mBó potatoes topped with dollops of
    home-made butter
Baby carrots and broccoli spears
Blackberries and rowanberries with clotted cream
Hand-made chocolates and truffles
Uisce beatha coffee.

"I have some non-alcoholic mead for you Aisling," he added. "What would you like for starters?"

"Rowanberries," she answered. "I love them." Servants, in long white linen tunics, filled yew dishes from the self-replenishing cauldron.

"It's *Imbolc*, our spring festival," the Daghda informed Aisling. "Spring festivals are celebrated all over the underworld universe."

"Yes," said Zeus. "We have a wonderful flower and dance festival back home. My daughter, Persephone, a three-in-one goddess with Demeter and Hecate, is carried below the earth every winter and rises again in spring."

"Just like the flowers," said Aisling, realizing that, although it seemed like yesterday, months had passed since her arrival in the underworld. "So this is how those three hundred years passed in Tír na nÓg," she mused.

In the distance Aisling heard chants:

Imbolc, Imbolc, winter has gone.
Imbolc, Imbolc, spring is in song.

They walked on through the woods. Seated on a tree stump, the god Oghma, dressed in a black leather tunic and black sandals, carved letters from a log. "Ogham is our written word," the Daghda informed her "and it records our sacred story for posterity."

"I am its creator," said Oghma, "my words are poetry." He handed the newly carved letter to the Daghda who blew on it. A bird skin formed around it, its heart fluttered and then it soared out of the Daghda's hand and flew away.

"Will it come back?" asked Aisling.

"No," said the Daghda. "When it finds a resting place, its bird skin will disintegrate and the Ogham letter will wait in hope for a caring passer-by to treasure it."

81

"I'll ask Miss Moore to set up a 'Rescue an Ogham Letter Society' when I get home," promised Aisling.

Oghma dipped his hand into a creel of letters and handed one to Aisling.

"Does this mean I have the gift of words?" she asked, thrilled to bits.

"Firstly, it must fly away, find a resting place and then you must search for and treasure it," replied Oghma.

They left him and walked on to another clearing where nine hazel trees formed a circle around a deep well. Boann told Aisling that anyone who ate these nuts received the gift of knowledge. Aisling stopped and ate some. "Knowledge is greatly prized here in the underworld," she reflected. Nearby, on a bed of cobblestones set deep in the ground, a gigantic fire hissed, crackled and spat, its flames leaping up into the sky. The Daghda's daughter Brigid, a goddess, with her inseparable sisters, danced around it. They were joined by nineteen fire maidens, each of whom had tended the fire for one day. Aisling watched in horror as Brigid leapt across the fire-pit, a column of fire from her hair burning up to the sky, flames leaping from her hands and fireballs from her fingers.

The maidens chanted:

Ancient fire
Inspire
New life
Into our mother
Earth.

Water from the sacred well was brought to Brigid. As she supped it, a column of smoke spiralled upwards out of her head and the flames and fireballs were quenched. Into the clearing, wearing an orange, satin cloak, which matched the gleaming strands of her long red hair, which glowed in the firelight, danced a three-in-one goddess. Gold serpentine bangles coiled around her wrists and ankles. She held a silver apple tree branch in her right hand.

"You see before you the maiden Morrigan," said Boann. The Morrigan turned to reveal her second aspect: "Creator mother," whispered Boann.

"Stunning!" exclaimed Aisling.

The Morrigan then let out a spine-chilling screech, leapt into the fire waving her silver apple branch, turned and faced the crowd. Aisling's stomach retched when she saw a filthy black-toothed hag, her limp hair matted, extend a gnarled hand to her.

"Step into the fire and make a wish," she shrieked.

"Must I?" Aisling whispered to Boann, shifting nervously from foot to foot.

"Take the apple branch," insisted the Morrigan. Aisling didn't dare refuse the foul-smelling hag. Hopefully her black shiny shoes would withstand the heat. She stepped onto the scorching coals.

"I wish, I wish to have No-Name's cap back," she said.

The silver apple branch flew out of her hand. Something fluttered through the air and landed on her head.

"No-Name," she called.

A thin column of smoke enveloped her and she floated upwards.

She looked down at the shocked faces of all present. What was it about No-Name that upset both gods and druids alike?

Chapter Thirteen

Fair exchange
is no robbery

nother mystery tour! *Pity I'm not a three-in-one girl,* she reflected. *Then I could send myself home to reassure them that I'm well, and my second self meanwhile could scout the underworld and check things out for my real self.* She landed close to a wicker basket, not unlike the one which had brought her to the underworld, and stepped in; the door closed and it travelled a little distance. The door slid open and there, bold as brass, was No-Name.

"At your service," he said with a shark-like grin.

"Get me out of here. I'm homesick."

No-Name threw back his head and laughed. "Darach, our herbalist, has a deadly homesickness remedy for you."

"Cyanide or Arsenic?" asked Aisling, who liked murder, mystery and suspense novels.

"Wait and see."

He tapped the tunnel walls and the passageway opened out into a kitchen in which were gleaming silver stoves, bronze ovens, and polished copper pots hanging from iron bars, along with oak dressers filled with sparkling silver and gold goblets and plates: everywhere buzzed with life. Little *lios* men and *lios* women hummed working tunes as they prepared chocolate truffles, emerald clusters and clover drops under the direction of a bouncing, energetic girl named Jenny, who had sleep-walked into a *lios sídhe* near Curramore and was taken directly to the *sídhe* kitchen. She rushed over to Aisling and No-Name, threw white linen tunics over their heads and told them to start stacking boxes of dolmen drops, will-of-the-wispies, toatie-oaties, mars mouthfuls, icy-spicies, lizard wizards, and caterpillar chillers on the waiting trams which ran like clockwork through the underworld. Tall, white rabbits scurried alongside, pulling heavy casks of mead to the *Imbolc* festival.

Once Jenny was out of sight, they discarded their tunics and hopped on an underworld tram which headed in the direction of Darach's herb garden. No-Name pushed Aisling out of the tram at an open gate where Darach, oblivious to all but himself, a black, woollen cap pulled down over his eyes, sat cross-legged in front of a stone slab, mixing herbs and muttering in low tones:

Daisy juice daily apply to sore eyes,
Boiled and cooled once, twice, thrice.
Dandelions cure all kidney aches
If mixed with a cube of our black ice.
Garlic crushed is good for the blood

It lowers the pressure when it's up.
To heal a rash on nose, throat or bum
Rub on some buttermilk with your left thumb.

"Great! I must remember the cure for sore eyes for Grandad," whispered Aisling to No-Name. Darach, who didn't seem to notice the peeping Toms, continued stirring and muttering:

If your lover lacks some zip
Press Lily of the Valley to his lips.
If he's too enthusiastic
Purple orchids will do the trick.
If upon your head you fall
Eat fresh violets, roots and all.
If your tooth is very sore
Lick a black snail's head and count to four.

He then swung around, glared at Aisling, and said: "A curse on thieving eavesdroppers. I heard your whispers about using my cure for your grandad's eyes."

"Cure. What cure?" exclaimed Aisling. "Miss Moore says I have a head like a sieve and dad calls me 'Little Miss Forgetful'."

"Is that so, Little Miss Prying Eyes?" asked Darach. "Now, where did I leave my stinging eye and ear-drops, which I use to treat prying eyes and cocked ears?"

"No! No stinging drops please," pleaded Aisling.

"Helleboraster Maximus then," said Darach, holding up a manky-looking thin glass tube, brimful of filthy yellow liquid. "It's a madness cure, Little Miss Eavesdropping Prying Eyes, and it's for you." He stood up. "Open wide," he commanded. Aisling's lips were clenched tight. He clicked his fingers and her lower jaw dropped instantly.

A scalding hot trickle of Helleboraster Maximus slid down her throat and exploded in the pit of her stomach. She had an urge to vomit, but didn't dare.

"So, what's my remedy for grandads sore eyes?" Darach asked.

"He has 20/20 vision," Aisling spluttered.

"Ten out of ten for Helleboraster Maximus," he said. "Now, what brings you here?"

"The home-sickness cure," said No-Name.

"Forget about it," said Aisling. "I'll survive. Let's not take up any more of Darach's precious time." She stuck her fingers in her ears to make sure she didn't overhear even a syllable as they made their way out.

They came to the mead kitchen where recipe charts hung on the walls.

"Noah's Mead is one of our oldest recipes," said No-Name, pointing out a chart. He filled a goblet. "Try some," he said.

Aisling sipped the sweet mead and liked it. She cast her eye around the kitchen. There were jars on shelves labelled dry, sweet, sparkling, rich and fruity mead. Green and purple glass tubes, filled with essences and perfumes extracted from eastern aromatic plants, flown there by the Asian *sídhe*, hung on chains from the ceiling. They were individually marked as follows: Marjoram, Tarragon, Liquorice, Henna, and Gentian, and used in the making of liqueurs.

Coriander, aniseed, juniper, bitter almonds, hazel nuts, and brazil nuts were stored in wicker baskets. Grape wines were stored in gigantic casks made from the oak trees in Coolatin forest. A gold cask contained what smelled and looked like brandy, Aisling's dad's favourite drink.

"*Eau de Vie de Vin*," No-Name informed her. "*Les Lutins de St Étienne* never fail to bring us a cask when making their annual visit. And here is our *pièce de résistence*, the famous Pliny wine. We stole the recipe from the cellars of the famous

Roman naturalist, Pliny the elder, thousands of years ago. And here is—"

Loud clattering and battering on the walls prevented him from finishing the sentence. It sounded like World War Three was breaking out.

An angry swarm of the *slua sídhe*, headed by Maebh, burst in on them, knocking down the wall charts. They descended like a mist around Aisling, lifted her on high and flew her back down the passageway to the treasure *lios*, dumped her unceremoniously on a table shaped like a crescent moon and interrogated her.

"Where is it?"

"Where have you hidden it?"

"What have you done with it?"

"It's our treasure and it belongs here."

"We know you took it."

They crowded around her menacingly, their faces taut with rage.

"You can forget about getting through the trap door. It's sealed. Don't even think about touching No-Name's cap or we'll chop off your head."

They asked question after endless question, not pausing to afford her the opportunity to reply. Aisling decided to fire a few questions back at them.

"Where is Fachtna's cell?"

"What have you done to him?"

"He's sojourning below the waves in a leaky, watery dungeon, awaiting court martial. Hand over Cúchulainn's golden ball and he'll get out."

"No. It's destined for the National Museum. It belongs to the children of Ireland."

"It belongs to us," hissed Maebh.

"It belongs to us," hissed the *sídhe*. "It belongs to us."

"Fachtna intends to hand it over to the museum as soon as we get out of here," said Aisling, her eyes flashing defiance.

"Will he now?" a seething Maebh sneered. "If he does, he will find himself a prize exhibit in the nearby National History Museum, stuffed to the gills like the giant elk and just as extinct. We are masters of the art of taxidermy."

Noting Aisling's stubborn jaw-line, she softened her tone of voice. "Come on, now. Have a little sense and tell us where you have hidden Cúchulainn's golden ball."

Aisling pursed her lips.

"Confess or we'll gut, fillet, and skin you alive and then, ever so slowly, roast you on our spit."

Aisling clenched her knuckles. "I'm no blabbermouth," she retorted. "I refuse to be bullied. For your information, we follow an anti-bullying code of conduct in our school."

"Well, you're not at school now and you're unlikely to be there again."

"I'm saying nothing," said Aisling.

"I'm saying nothing," mimicked a sneering Maebh.

"I'm saying nothing," mimicked the *sídhe*. "I'm saying nothing."

"We have ways of making you talk," Maebh threatened. "Let's fetch the instruments of torture for our very own Deirdre of the Sorrows."

"Yippee! Yippee!" shouted the *sídhe* in glee. "Can we all have a go at torturing her?"

"Yes, one at a time, in an orderly line, after me."

They swarmed into the air and flew out through the treasure *lios* walls. Aisling tried to get off the table but her bum was stuck to it.

In through the window flew the magpie, carrying in its beak a gold torc which it put on a shelf.

"You still here?" it asked.

"Yes and no," answered Aisling.

"I see you're moonstruck, or should I say moon-stuck," quipped the magpie. It perched on her shoulder for a few moments and then flew around the *lios* peering behind couches and under tables.

"Lost something?" asked Aisling.

"I don't suppose you know the whereabouts of Cúchulainn's golden ball?"

"And I don't suppose you know the whereabouts of grandad Aonghus' gold fob watch and chain?" she asked.

"*Touché!* Let's not draw swords. We could exchange the fob watch and chain for Cúchulainn's golden ball."

"No deal!" said Aisling. "I thought you'd have realized by now that Cúchulainn's golden ball is *not* a negotiable issue."

"Maebh will be back any second," said the magpie. "What will you do then?"

Aisling furrowed her brow. Grandad would be thrilled to have his watch back. But how, she wondered, could she tempt the magpie to part with it. The answer struck her like a bolt from the blue. Seeds! Magpies love seeds.

"Seeds of knowledge from the druid's grove," she said, "in exchange for grandad's fob watch and chain."

"A little knowledge is a dangerous thing," retorted the magpie.

"Tasty seeds!" she persisted.

"Go on then!" The magpie flapped its wings in glee. "You drive a hard bargain," it said, opening wide its beak. Aisling popped in three seeds.

"Yum, yum," said the magpie. "Any more where they came from?"

"Fob watch and chain," she insisted. He handed it over and she stitched it into the hem of her skirt with her Ariadne needle and thread and tapped it invisible with her blackthorn stick.

"Get me out of here and you'll have three more tasty seeds," she said.

"That's a tall order!"

"If you don't want them, I'll eat—"

"I do, I do," said the magpie, circling the table three times.

"Hurry," said Aisling, "before that mob returns."

"My seeds first," said the magpie, with a beady eye on her hand.

Aisling popped the three remaining seeds into its beak.

"You're in luck, your bum's unstuck," said the magpie. "Just tap yourself invisible, hop up on my back and we'll away."

They flew out the latticed window just as Maebh and her *slua* burst in, firing arrows everywhere. The magpie dropped her back to the mead kitchen.

Chapter Fourteen

bubbles galore: a cocktail party with a difference

"**Y**ou escaped," said No-Name, his bushy eyebrows rising with surprise "I'm impressed," he added, giving her the thumbs–up sign, "but be warned: you're in double trouble for double-crossing Maebh. She has, in all likelihood, reserved your seat on death row with the others."

"She'll have to catch me first."

"Don't underestimate Maebh. Death row is located at the bottom of the ocean in Manannán's palace. It would be easier to escape from Alcatraz than from there."

"Your cap will keep me safe down here in the underworld."

"That's where you're mistaken. My cap has no protective powers in Manannán's watery dungeons."

"You're joking!"

"I most definitely am not. Manannán, son of Lir, god of the sea, is not one of us. He lives beyond the ninth wave. When the Tuatha Dé Danann were defeated by the Milesians at the battles of Tailteann and Mis, we, the *sídhe*, took refuge in the hills. It was Manannán who advised us on how to organize ourselves. He mapped out each *sídhe* hill under a High King, gave us the gift of invisibility and proposed we elect for ourselves a sovereign ruler in the full expectation that we would elect Lir, his father. Fionnbharr, Oonagh, and Maebh supported Lir, but we chose our own Bobh Dearg as high king. Manannán stormed off in disgust. He and his wife, Fand, have remained hostile to us ever since, although they have retained links with Fionnbharr, Oonagh, and Maebh. Manannán is the recipient of many gifts from their treasure *lios* and he reciprocates with gifts from his home beyond the magical boundary which separates our world and his. Enbarr, his sea horse, is at their disposal at all times. His sea dungeons are renowned all over the *sídhe* universe. You would be wise to hand back your ill-gotten goods to Maebh before you find yourself in deep water. Incidentally, your grandmother and Fachtna could be in one of his padded cells."

"Then, even if there's only the slightest chance to help them escape, you've got to help me get there."

"Don't talk nonsense. No one gets out of there. Maebh, in all probability, is plotting a few treats for you in Manannán's torture chamber. We would be well advised to take precautions to out-manoeuvre her."

"*You're* going to help *me*. Why?"

"I, not you Miss Klepto, shall ultimately be held responsible by Maebh for Cúchulainn's missing ball."

"Let's scupper her plans to nab me. There must be something here we could use to put her off scent."

"Mmm. We could throw her a little cocktail party. Fetch some goblets and bring them here," No-

Name said, tucking his bushy beard into his belt. "Maebh and her mob never resist a drink. They like to wet their whistles."

"You mean—get them drunk?"

"Well, maybe a tiddly bit tipsy." No-Name, usually as cagey as a feral cat, impetuously selected the largest copper pot in the kitchen and put it on the stove.

"Fetch a ladle and pour some Dianchecht's draught into this."

"What's that?"

"A 365-herb miracle cure if administered in carefully measured units, but something that will bring about a disorientating, nerve-racking condition if taken in unmeasured quantities. Don't be shy," he encouraged her. "Fling it all in, if you like." Aisling did so and No-Name brought the draught to the boil before letting it simmer on a low heat.

"Now," he ordered, "Fetch some Elzeimer juice and a few scoops of herbs marked 'Dangerous in Large Doses' and stir them well into our *sídhe*-babe trap while I head off to fetch some Helleboraster Maximus from Darach."

Soon the copper pot was rumbling, gurgling and spewing sparks. No-Name returned and, throwing all caution to the wind, poured an entire bottle of Helleboraster Maximus into it. Aisling asked if she could add in some *Vin de Vénus*.

"Great idea!" he said, with a glint in his eye. "Venusian grapes, from which *Vin de Vénus* is made, are hot enough to melt tin, zinc, and lead, so they'll set Maebh's belly on fire. Fling in a generous ladle-full and try a little drop yourself while you're at it. It's perfectly safe in small quantities." He offered her a small thimbleful.

"Er, no than—"

"Take it," he insisted, putting it into her hand.

Just then there was a loud banging on the kitchen wall. Aisling got such a fright that she spilled the contents of the thimble on her shoes. They sizzled, levitated off the floor and she fell backwards and bashed her head off the flagstones. The door burst open. Eight white rabbits rushed in with a long trolley.

"We've come for the mead," said Coinín.

"You have arrived in the nick of time. We have an emergency here. Help me lift Aisling onto the trolley and we'll bring her to Doctor Cnámh Sídhe."

"But—but—" protested Coinín.

"There will be a small cask of mead for your good self later," said No-Name.

"Your word is my command," replied Coinín, eyeing the mead.

They lifted an unconscious Aisling onto the trolley and sped off with her just as Maebh and her *sídhe*-babes burst in. They helped themselves to goblets and guzzled every drop from the copper pot until they collapsed on the floor, blowing air bubbles galore and sending smoke signals out their nostrils.

Chapter Fifteen

The Bróigín trademark, and, of course, a tribunal

The eight tall rabbits, led by Coinín, arrived at Doctor Cnámh Sídhe's surgery, followed by a breathless No-Name. A note pinned on the surgery door read: At Cobbler's Tribunal. Coinín spun the trolley around and they raced to the courtroom.

"Shhh! Shhh!" The porter put his fingers to his lips.

"But we have an emergency," protested Coinín, who was anxious to get back to the kitchen for the cask of mead.

A voice boomed: "Order in the court! Order in the court!"

"The judge is giving his address," explained the porter, glancing down at Aisling. "She is scheduled to give her testimony later."

"Aisling is in no fit state for that," protested No-Name.

"Shhh! Shhh!"

The voice boomed on: "Every leipreachán in these *leasanna* and forts must give an account of his activities in the weeks before the Imbolc. Some not-so-smart *leipreachán* made a right botch of Queen Bébo's new boots, our Bróigín trademark is tarnished and our reputation

97

in tatters. The queen of the Land of Lupra and Luprachán has developed an ugly corn on her baby toe, and is barred from ruling her subjects until this physical deformity is removed. Iubhdán, the king, is furious. It's an annus horribilis for the royal family. Eisirt, the royal bard, has composed a satire on the Bróigín trademark. We are the laughing stock of the Association of Bróigín Traders. A Lupra-Luprachánian invasion is imminent. The rogue *leipreachán* in our midst must be exposed. Lawyers at extortionist rates have been engaged to represent us. Heads will roll!" He paused.

A second voice roared: "Order in the court! Order in the court! Dr Cnámh Sídhe to the stand."

No-Name whispered to the porter, "When he has completed his evidence, may I ask him to look at Aisling." The porter nodded his head.

"Do you swear to tell the truth, the whole truth and nothing but the truth?"

"I do."

"Speak," said the judge.

"I have examined the royal corn which Queen Bébo attributes to our sub-standard boots. A triple by-pass of the small toe cornio is urgently required, in short, open toe surgery."

The packed courtroom gasped and held its breath. There was nervous coughing.

"You may step down, Dr Cnámh Sídhe," said the judge. "I call for a recess during which three-way mirrors are to be strategically positioned so that each one of us shall have a view of exhibit one, Queen Bébo's corn, and that alone."

The doors were flung open and the judge, in grey wig and black gown, swept out, followed by the doctor. No-Name stepped forward. "Pardon the intrusion, but would you be so good as to take a look at this patient."

"Bring her to my surgery," instructed the doctor. "We do not approve of patients on trolleys in corridors. It's most unprofessional."

The rabbits raced to the surgery and gingerly lifted Aisling on to the day-bed and raced off again.

"A thimbleful of *Vin de Vénus* spilled accidentally on her shoes," explained No-Name.

Dr Cnámh Sídhe instructed his nurse to remove them for dry-cleaning. He sniffed: "A simple enough case of foot and fumes. I shall amputate her feet after the tribunal."

A horrified No-Name gasped. "She must be punished for using our precious *Vin de Vénus* as shoe spray," added the doctor. "But perhaps amputating her feet is a trifle drastic." No-Name looked relieved.

"Nurse," called the doctor, "Fetch six drops of *sídhe* smelling salts, three to be inserted into each nostril, and when she surfaces, sit with her at the back of the courtroom."

The nurse followed orders. Aisling was a little wobbly on her feet as she got down from the day-bed. "Best hurry back. They're waiting for you. You're the key witness," the nurse said.

"That's news to me," said Aisling.

"We are always a step ahead of you," a smug-faced No-Name told her as they returned to the courtroom where they sat quietly with the tribunal reporters.

Teams of thin, pale-faced, long-nosed *leipreacháin* occupied the seats. They wore red cocked hats, red swallow-tailed jackets with gold buttons down the middle, green knee-breeches, and long black boots with curled up toes. Each team had an appointed spokesperson. Queen Bébo reclined on a red, white and blue *chaise longue*, her naked foot held aloft by a red-faced Iubhdán. Her hair was standing on end, causing her crown to wobble ungraciously. Her teeth were clenched, as were her fists, and her imperial eyes blazed with fury. The reporters from the Times had their quills to hand.

"Gold-digger to the stand," called the clerk of the court.

"Do you swear to tell the truth, the whole truth, and nothing but the truth?"

"I do."

"You are charged with supplying sub-standard boots to the Land of Lupra and Luprachán. How do you plead?"

"Not guilty," answered Gold-digger. "My team and I were otherwise engaged when the said order was being processed,

excavating gold in the Wicklow hills near the Dargle, as our reserves were depleted. During the weeks preceding Imbolc we were busy gouging," he paused momentarily to unpick the contents of his nose, "hacking and chiselling out sufficient gold to replenish our crocks of gold at rainbow's end."

"Innocent of all charges Gold-digger, you may step down."

Next to take the stand was Euros-a-Plenty.

"Do you swear to tell the truth, the whole truth and nothing but the truth?"

"I do."

"How do you plead?"

"Not guilty. During the weeks in question, my team and I were busy from dusk to dawn gifting good folk above with our inexhaustible purses, *sparáin scillinge* as they were called in the old days. We hid them under pillows, in schoolbags, on window ledges, and in kitchen cupboards. I myself looked after Pertie who doesn't turn his nose up at a few bob, even though gifts must be declared to the proper authorities. I was about to put 50 brand new euro notes into the bowl under his bed, but decided against it in case he was caught short during the night and needed to shed a tear for the patriots. Instead, I popped our finest *sparán* into his safe and watched from the window ledge as *the most devious of all* opened the *sparán*, counted the notes, rubbed his manicured hands in glee, stuttering:

"An–an–an–anudder fifty grand to change into dollars, back to euros and den to sterling". Then I went back to the workshop, happy that my mission was accomplished."

"You may step down, Euros-a-Plenty. I declare you innocent."

Hobnail was next to take the oath. "It was stocktaking time for us. I and my team were busy counting, sorting, sharpening, repairing and buffing up all pincers, nip and tuckers, feather and buffing knives, bradawls, fenders, lap-irons, hob-nails, nuts, bolts, rivets, and stirrups in our ironmongery.

We worked two shifts, without as much as a blue-flu or a screw-up."

There was a chuckle from the courtroom.

"You may step down Hobnail. I declare you innocent."

Cross-stitch was then sworn in. "My cross-stitchers and I were busy during the period in question, knitting, darning, crocheting, turning the toes and heels of our Lupra and Luprachán annual order for, as everyone knows, one doesn't wear old stockings in new brogues. We were joined by apprentices from La Lutinerie de St Étienne. We executed plain and purl, cables and knots to the tune of the *Marseillaise*, taking as our role models the French knitting ladies who clicked their needles to the chop, chop, chop of the guillotine in 1789."

"Step down, Cross-stitch. I declare you innocent of all charges."

Bend-Over-Backwards took the stand. "My team and I were busy bending over backwards, side and arse-ways, keeping the workshops spick and span. We were at the beck and call of the gold-diggers, Euros-a-Plenty, hob-nailers, cross-stitchers, ironmongers, *haut*-and low-*couturiers* and apprentices of all grades and levels. Our newly commissioned Póg mo Thóns and little Tóinín le Talamh were fetching, carrying, segregating and recycling all slivers, quivers, residues, scraps and droppings, down to the smallest pinhead."

"Step down, Bend-over-Backwards. You are innocent."

Next to the stand was Labhraidh who had chosen the Bróigín trademark for the *leipreachán* industry. It was he who personally designed and made Aisling's black patent shoes. He sported a Charvet shirt and mohair suit, as befits aristocracy. He laughed before taking the oath, "Haw-haw-haw, hee-hee-hee".

"One haw-hee is enough," said the judge gruffly. "Guilty or not guilty?"

"Exactly," said Labhraidh.

"Exactly what?" asked the judge, his taut lips quivering in exasperation.

"I am either guilty or not guilty of all charges?"

Bébo's nostrils flared and her jaws tightened as she wriggled her small toe at him.

"I take none or all of the responsibility for the ill-fitting brogues," Labhraidh said. "Templates of the royal feet were sent to me from King Iubhdán and Queen Bébo's Land of Lupra and Luprachán from which, using the softest calf skin, I personally cut and hand-stitched the brogues. Fortunately, I have retained the templates for future royal Twinkle Toe orders. I call for her Highness's brogues to be examined forthwith. If all boot angles, corners, twists and turns correspond exactly to the templates supplied to me, I am not guilty. If however, the templates used, which have inflicted this gross deformity on the queen and prevented her from holding high office, were deliberately incorrectly cut, then one of her own Luprácháin is guilty of high treason."

"Let exhibit two, the template, and exhibit three, the royal brogue, be measured against exhibit one, the corny royal foot," ordered the judge.

"I ask your worship to also consider the possibility that jealous up-starts from the Land of Lupra and Luprachán are endeavouring to squeeze us *leipreacháin* out of the shoe trade by tarnishing our good reputation," added Labhraidh. "Rogue traders we are not. Our standards are unparalleled as my next witness Aisling shall testify."

"Aisling, take the stand, please."

No-Name pushed a bewildered Aisling out of her seat. She was duly sworn in. "Who designed and made the shoes you are wearing?"

"Labhraidh."

"Labhraidh who exactly?"

"Labhraidh *leipreachán,* whose handicraft bears the Bróigín trademark."

"Do the shoes fit?"

"Like a glove, your honour, if you'll pardon the pun."

The judge's icy stare sliced through her. "No further questions. Would counsel for Queen Bébo like to cross-examine either of these witnesses?"

All eyes were riveted on Queen Bébo and King Iubhdán as their senior counsel whispered to them.

"My clients withdraw all charges." All in the courtroom gasped in disbelief.

King Iubhdán dropped Bébo's naked leg. She pulled on her stocking with one hand, settled her wobbly crown with the other and, muttering gibberish, fled the courtroom, followed by King Iubhdán, their senior counsel, the royal entourage, the *Lupra Press* and *Sleeveen Times* reporters and photographers. They streamed out onto the lawns into an awaiting heliumcopter.

"I declare you not guilty of all charges, Labhraidh," said the judge.

All in the courtroom cheered as they rushed out on the lawns just in time to see the heliumcopter zoom away.

"Back to the workshops," Labhraidh ordered the *leipreacháin*.

"Can I come too?" said Aisling.

"My pleasure," said Labhraidh.

They crossed the lawns through double oak doors into a huge stone workshop. In the centre of the entrance hall there was an enormous gold disc displaying twenty-two concentric circles around its perimeter and seven indentations in its centre. A flying saucer-like object was parked on it.

"What's this?" Aisling screwed up her face and peered at it.

"Saturn," replied Labhraidh. "This is our saturnellite, commissioned by the Greek and Roman gods and goddesses, and made by Mercury and Hermes to Archimedes' design. It carries our export orders all over the *sídhe* universe, first class."

"Let's hop on," Aisling said to No-Name.

"What about the workshop?"

"Another time, cross my heart," Aisling promised as she hopped onto the saturnellite.

"Come on," she shouted at No-Name.

"You're wasting your time," Labhraidh said with a snigger. "The take-off code is top secret."

"Cracking codes is a hobby of mine," said Aisling, confidently examining the keypad inside and noting the column of double consonants.

"Mmm, let me think," she said, putting her brain into top gear. "A disc with 22 concentric circles encircling 7 indentations = $^{22}/_7$. Pi," she shouted triumphantly. "Look for the Pi symbol, π," she said to No-Name. "It resembles two linked Ts."

"Found it," he shouted triumphantly. "Hold on tight."

Chapter Sixteen

Power play and politics

Da-va-voom! The saturnellite shot upwards so fast, Aisling almost fell off. No-Name grabbed one of her legs as she stumbled.

"Hang on," she yelled. "I don't fancy freefall."

He yanked her up. When she had regained her composure, he pointed to a gold disc displaying a list of destinations.

> Dana's Grove.
> Mount Olympus.
> Land of Lupra and Luprachán.
> Lutinerie de St Étienne.

"This Dana must be very important. Fionnbharr proposed a toast to her at his banquet," Aisling remarked.

"Dana," he said, in his usual matter-of-fact tone of voice, "is mother of all the gods. Her hair is spun from sunlight and her skin is as pale as the moon. Her turquoise blue mantle protects the earth and all on it. Her three-pronged silver spiral brooch emits a high pitched, ultra-sonic sound that can paralyse any opponent, whether earthen, otherworld or alien."

"Maybe she would help me rescue Fachtna."

"Dana can't abandon her duties at the drop of a hat to go on some wild goose chase to Manannán's dungeons, which by the way, are as impregnable as Fort Knox," No-Name informed her. "Our underworld is pyramidal and Dana's word is law."

"Where are you No-Namers on this pyramid?"

"Level 7."

"And Dana?"

"Dana, the gods and goddesses are at Level 1."

"So, you No-Namers are at rock bottom?"

"Yes." No-Name blushed. His jaws protruded as he spat back, "Doesn't mean we're stupid and you can pull the wool over our eyes." He fixed her with a steely stare. "Where did you hide Cúchulainn's ball?" he asked.

Aisling fingered her blackthorn stick. "Finder keeps, looser weeps," she scoffed. "I reckon Dana's three-pronged silver spiral brooch would come in handy too," she teased.

No Name glared daggers at her." Don't even think about it," he said.

"So you No-Namers are at rock bottom," she repeated. "I bet you share your space with card-sharks and gamblers. No wonder the Druids hate your guts, trespassing on their land."

"That does it." No-Name had "that Machiavellian look" in his eye, which Aisling's dad often attributed to her mother Jackie. "Odds on you lose that cap again," he sneered. "Let me know when you decide where you want to go on this saturnellite," he said, changing the subject.

"I want to go to Dana's grove."

No-Name pressed the appropriate button and sent a telepathic message to Dana requesting permission to see her along with a guest. The saturnellite did a 180-degree U-turn and then veered right, cannon-balling through the sky at incredible speeds, and finally losing height as it plunged downwards and hovered over a field in which Aisling noticed a grassy mound. It tilted sideways, allowing them to slide off easily. No-Name told Aisling to eat some sloes and haws which grew nearby, while he went ahead and tapped on Dana's door with his blackthorn stick. It opened and he dropped to his knees in a respectful gesture.

"Arise, No-Name," said Dana, touching him lightly on the head. "What brings you here?"

"Aisling needs your help to rescue her friend, Fachtna, from Manannán's dungeon and her grandmother, Bláithín, too, if she's there. I have been assigned to her during her stay here."

"I promised not to go home without Fachtna," Aisling explained.

"What makes you think that I can help?" asked Dana, leading them briskly into a vaulted room filled with wall tapestries, baskets of flowers and a spinning wheel. Aisling, who knew that she was in dire need of *sidhe* inspiration, said a prayer to Bláithín and heard herself answer: "As Mother of the Universe, it is your duty to care equally for human and *sidhe*."

Dana's eyes twinkled. "And," she added. "What's the most important lesson you have ever learned."

Aisling thought long and hard. "The absence of evidence of the *sidhe* is not evidence of their absence," she spoke slowly and deliberately.

Dana raised her ash wand, tapped Aisling on each shoulder and said: "I, Dana, Mother of the Universe, herewith anoint you honorary member of the Ancient Order of the *Sídhe*."

Aisling was taken aback at this unexpected honour and fumbled for appropriate words. "Uh huh." She waited for more inspiration. "Er—th—thanks," she stammered, "does that mean you'll help?"

"Yes," Dana replied. "It's time Manannán and I settled a few old scores. He is a stormy god and a powerful adversary. He and treasure-mad Maebh are allies. Manannán upends ships at Murúch's rock and swops his ill-gotten gains with his sea god friends Poseidon and Neptune. His daughters Sheelin, Ennel, Owel, and Derrevaragh entice young men below the waves with their enchanting sea shanties and use them as playthings. He has strong links with the Neptunites, and his wife—Fand—and Amphitrite—Neptune's wife—are best friends."

Dana sat at her spinning wheel. "Fetch me some purple foxgloves from the woods," she said to Aisling "and I shall weave them with this silk thread into protective capes and bootees for the watery realms. We had better move quickly before Manannán exchanges your friend Fachtna for a foreign hostage." On seeing Aisling's horrified expression she added, "or worse." Aisling sped off and returned with the completed order. "Work as quickly as you can," she implored. When the capes and bootees were ready, Dana handed them over. She also gave both No-Name and Aisling a blue lapis lazuli stone very like the one she wore on her brow.

"The lapis lazuli is the stone of truth and friendship, Aisling," said Dana. "It offers protection from physical danger and psychic attacks, which it recognizes, blocks and returns to their source."

Dana, Aisling and No-Name went outside where two piebald stallions awaited them. Dana rode one and Aisling sat behind No-Name on the other. They raced across land to the sea-shore and galloped into a cave where seven times seven steps led down into dark tunnels. The only faint light to be seen was Dana's halo which cast a glow all around. On they raced until, in the distance, Aisling heard a faint ratatata, ratatata, ratatata.

"Sounds like a tram," Aisling said. "I never expected to see a tram here."

"Our architects and engineers, helped by Epeius who designed the famous Trojan horse, designed and made this tram for our submarine excursions," explained Dana.

The tram arrived. The stallions halted and their riders dismounted.

"It's a miniature version of the tram in the Transport Museum in Howth," exclaimed Aisling.

"It will bring us to Murúch's rock," explained Dana.

They stepped on and Dana took the controls. Aisling ran up and down the stairs and had fun flicking the seats forwards and backwards. Eventually it stopped, the door opened, they got out and walked up seven times seven stone steps until they were right under the chunnel tunnel's roof. They put on their foxglove and silk capes and bootees. Dana tapped the tunnel roof with her ash wand, a trap door opened and they floated out into uncharted waters. Giant sea perch, tiger and squirrel fish, red snapper, burr, spiny bat, elephant nose, and cat fish all swam around Manannán's sea garden.

Two green-eyed, shimmering sea-janitors in sea-green scaly uniforms, navy knee-high boots, and peaked caps guarded the entrance to his white marble palace. As they approached, the janitors swam forward to arrest them. Dana waved her ash wand and upended them.

"Bottoms up! Bottoms up!" sneered No-Name as they floated past the infuriated janitors, who had to doff their caps respectfully. Dana tapped on the gold door of Manannán's sea palace with her ash wand. It opened and they floated in. Tiny *sídhe* flitted here and there, strewing miniature trefoils on the gleaming white marble floor. Clusters of South-Sea pearls hung from the ivory ceiling. At the bottom of the entrance hall loomed huge double doors made of yew, over which, carved in gold, were the words "Manannán's Banqueting Room". Aisling held her breath.

Chapter Seventeen

A Repossession Order, telepathy, and extra-terrestrials

Oana tapped and they entered. A coral ceiling overlooked a carpet of purple, violet, and blue sea anemones on which an ornate gold table was laden with silver and bronze plates, filled to overflowing with sea fruits and delicacies and purple decanters filled with sea-wine. Little *murúcha* swam in and out through open-latticed windows and huge plants in earthenware pots climbed up the white marble walls and coiled their leaves around seascapes painted in marine water-colours. A green and black marble staircase led to an upper balcony.

Voices sounded in the distance. Manannán, greatly feared sea god, in greenish, translucent cape and black high-heeled wellington boots, eyes blazing fire and brimstone at the strangers, walked down the marble stairway, followed by his four daughters, Sheelin, Ennel, Owel, and Derravaragh. He bellowed in such fury that the nine-stringed harp slung over his shoulder in a diamond-studded, otter skin bag, played harsh discordant notes.

Several sea guards arrived on the scene with handcuffs and chains. Dana laughed as they did their utmost to take them prisoner and failed.

Manannán clicked his fingers. A fine-mesh, silver net floated down from the balcony and snared them. "It's my turn to laugh," Manannán jeered. "Peekaboo, my tangled trio."

"Peekabye." Dana touched the mesh with her brow and, to Manannán's fury, they floated out.

He bellowed again. A mighty sea dragon, breathing fire and smoke, emerged from under the anemones and coiled around their legs. Dana bent over and touched its tail with her lapis lazuli. Instantly it howled with rage and released them.

Manannán, making a supreme effort to soften his thunderous facial expression, suggested coaxingly: "Let's quit our games, and be civil. Allow me take your capes and bootees and you shall partake of our seafood platter and full-bodied Zanzibar wine."

"Will Fand be joining us?" asked Dana.

"My dear wife and her best friend, Amphitrite, are on a shopping spree at the sea emporium and just as well, as she would pale into insignificance beside your loveliness."

"*Plámás* will get you nowhere," said Dana coldly. "We have not come to dine. We are here on a mission."

"Mission Impossible," sneered Manannán. His daughters giggled.

Dana ignored the jibe. She withdrew from her cloak a parchment scroll tied with a red ribbon and opened it out for all to see the words "Repossession Order".

"This is a legal and binding document," she said, "which sets out my rights as goddess of the land and all that is on it."

"In these watery realms, you have no rights!" roared Manannán. "I have not forgotten that long ago, when you all slunk away, defeated by the Milesians, I answered your call for assistance, set up your *sídhe* and gave you the gift of invisibility. All I expected in return was for my father, Lir, to be your elected supreme ruler, but you chose Bobh Derg, one of your own."

"You, Manannán, are an opportunist, and would, in time, have succeeded your father. We appreciated your help but we also recognized that you hoped to set yourself up as god of land and sea, which would have been disastrous, not only for us, the *sídhe*, but for all human kind." She pointed to the scroll. "This document sets out my rights as goddess of the land and all that's on it, including," she raised her voice an octave, "your palace."

Manannán threw back his head and laughed. "In these watery realms I am god and my word is law."

"Steady on there! Your palace is built on my land, the sea floor," Dana replied. "The ocean alone is yours."

Manannán curled his lips in an ugly sneer. "So," he said, "you have come to repossess your ocean floor and intend to give the god of the sea his marching orders." He winked at his daughters. "You, Dana, and whose army?"

"The first regiment of our highly trained *sídhe* rangers," replied Dana, eyeballing him.

Manannán shrieked with laughter. Sheelin, Ennel, Owel, and Derravaragh laughed too, but a little nervously.

"I shall send Enbharr and an advance party of *my* sea rangers to welcome your *sídhe* rangers," he sneered. "Think about it; *sídhe* rangers, sea rangers on the sea floor. Tell me, will they slip in indiscreetly, dressed in military-style foxglove capes and bootees like your good selves? See how I tremble."

"We have no need of your Enbharr," Dana said, winking at Aisling. "We have our own horse, a Trojan horse. Perhaps the sea god and his daughters would like to see it?" She knew they wouldn't resist the offer as sea gods are most inquisitive by nature.

"Why not?" said Manannán. "A Trojan horse on our own doorstep!"

"Yes, a finer specimen by far than your Enbharr! Our horse has iron lungs."

"Never," said Manannán curling up his nose in disbelief.

"Follow me," said Dana, floating out into the hallway into Murúch's ocean which was teeming with one-eyed, fifteen-foot tall, finned humanoid creatures, Chinese dragon-like sea folk with goat and sheep heads, and leering, bubble-blubbering, snake-like fish.

When they arrived at the special entrance to the chunnel-tunnel, Dana took out her wand and tapped the waters.

"Divining?" Manannán jeered. His daughters clapped his witticism. They were so caught up with themselves that they failed to notice that the trap door had opened and that they were floating down the stone steps into the tunnel. The trap door closed behind them with a bang. Manannán let out a shriek. "What have you done with my water?" he roared.

"Shhh." Dana put a finger to her lips. "Listen!" The ratatata, ratatata was clearly approaching. "Here comes my Trojan horse."

The tram chugged into sight, the doors opened and three thousand *sídhe* soldiers, as in Virgil's famous account of the Trojan War, jumped out and surrounded Manannán and his daughters.

"Water, I can't live without water," gasped Manannán, who was weakening as fast as his beautiful daughters were wilting.

"Arrest them all," Dana instructed the captain of the regiment, "and bring them to my dungeon for a taste of their own medicine."

"Water, water," gasped Manannán.

"Play us a little *goltraí* on that harp of yours," said Dana mockingly. "When you are all safely incarcerated, the *sídhe* orchestra will lull you to sleep with a *suantraí* while our *sídhe* soldiers make amorous advances to your lovely daughters."

"I shall never allow that," said Manannán. "Tell me what you want of us."

Dana tapped the repossession order with her quill which she had dipped in oak gall that morning.

"Sign above the wavy line," she ordered, offering it to Manannán, "you and your lovely daughters, then vacate my sea floor before it's too late."

Manannán hesitated. "But my palace is on the sea floor," he protested.

"Tough!" said Dana, "the sea floor and all that's on it is mine."

"Sign, daddy," pleaded Sheelin, Ennel, Owel, and Derravaragh.

"I'll sign," said Manannán, "but only if you promise to open the trap door a fraction so that I can catch my breath. You can keep your poisoned plume," he said, taking out a peacock's feather which had been dipped in octopus ink. "Open the trap door," he gasped, "before it's too late."

"You'd better not be up to any old tricks," said Dana tapping the trap door. "Sign," she said.

Manannán took a deep breath and signed, as did his daughters.

"I am a generous god," said Manannán with a sneer. The trap door burst fully open and a swarm of bat-like, two-footed, silver-suited creatures carrying tridents, paraglided in and surrounded Dana, No-Name and Aisling, and pinned them against the chunnel walls.

Neptune, the great sea god wearing a green scaly suit and slippers and carrying an enormous three-pronged trident towered over them. Aisling was terrified.

"Stay calm," whispered Dana. "I am more than a match for them. Remain focused and remember, you are the first human eyewitness to these extra-terrestrials." She beamed her three-pronged triple spiral brooch at the Neptunites. It emitted paralysing beams of light which disorientated Neptune and his minions and almost melted their tridents. As they howled with rage, the spiral brooch emitted three ultra-sonic, discordant notes which almost ruptured their eardrums.

"Do your worst," Dana ordered her *sídhe* regiment.

The three thousand rangers about-turned, surrounded the Neptunites and cemented their feet to the ground with a fast-fix mixture.

"Please, daddy, promise her a special gift," pleaded Derra-varagh. "I'm tired and I want to go home."

"Can some of these guys come back with us?" asked Sheelin, perking up and giving the handsome Neptunites the glad-eye.

Manannán glared at her. He turned to Dana, "You'll get your gift when I get home," he said quietly.

Dana turned to the captain of the *sídhe* rangers, "A Trojan job," she commended him, "well done." She handed him her lapis lazuli. "Set the Neptunites free," she ordered.

The *sídhe* captain released the crestfallen Neptunites and escorted them through the trap door where Neptune's sea horses awaited them and they rode home over the waves.

"Company dismissed," said the *sídhe* captain to his rangers. The Trojan horse flexed its muscles and filled its lungs with tunnel air, the tram doors opened and the *sídhe* army sat inside. The doors closed and, with a ratatata, ratatata, ratatata, it sped back down the tunnel.

Chapter Eighteen

Clóicíní Draíochta,
Sídhe-mail, and
the World Wide Web

Dana, No-Name and Aisling, followed by a subdued Manannán and his daughters returned to the palace. The sea janitors bowed to Dana and stepped aside, for it was clear from Manannán's demeanour that the goddess of the land had triumphed over the god of the sea.

Dana ordered Manannán to set the prisoners free. There was loud weeping and wailing from Sheelin, Ennel, Owel and Derravaragh as many handsome young Irish men were escorted to sea chariots and brought home to Ireland's shores and their loved ones.

Fachtna ran into the banqueting room shouting for joy. Aisling whispered into his ear as she hugged him. He clapped his hands in glee.

Dana accepted Manannán's offer of a glass of Zanzibar wine and Aisling and Fachtna tucked into delicious fairycakes, mini-chocolate éclairs and Turkish delight. They were caught off-guard when Maebh and her *slua sídhe* swarmed in.

"I see, Manannán, you have visitors," Maebh remarked, before catching sight of Fachtna, who was stuffing himself with chocolate éclairs. "Why is he unfettered?" she shrieked in rage.

"The prisoners have been set free on my instructions," said Dana.

"Is this true?" a disbelieving Maebh asked Manannán.

"Yes, more or less," he replied, sheepishly.

"Manannán, the chess grandmaster, has capitulated under the queen of the land's gambit, which makes you, Maebh, a disposable pawn down here, so sling your hook. I'll summon you later to my grove where you'll reap your just rewards," Dana said, as Aisling and Fachtna cheered.

"The game isn't over until checkmate," said a furious Manannán. "I shall have my sea architects and engineers design and build a floating palace. The god of the sea may have lost this battle but war has not yet commenced."

"Well said!" Maebh smiled approvingly at him. Then, catching sight of No-Name, she scowled. "No-Name, you'll come with me," she snarled.

"No-Name is under my protection," interjected Dana. "Leave now."

"I'll get even with you two yet, mark my words." Maebh shook her fist defiantly at Aisling and Fachtna. "Go stew in your own importance," Aisling jeered, as she and her *slua sídhe* stormed off.

"Time for my overdue gift," Dana said to Manannán. He placed two acorns on the palm of her hand.

"Is this a joke?"

"Nope! These acorns contain invisibility cloaks, just like my own cloak of mists."

"Harry Potter invisibility cloaks!" exclaimed Aisling and Fachtna in one voice.

"Who is this Potter who dares lay claim to my cloak of mists?" bellowed a furious Manannán. "Invisibility is mine since time began. I rendered the Tuatha Dé Danann invisible when they took refuge in the *sídhe*. My cloak is the veil between the visible and invisible worlds. It protects the well of wisdom which contains all otherworld knowledge. Harry Potter! If I get my hands on him I'll wring his bloody—"

"Potter is no threat to you, Manannán," Dana said reassuringly.

"The cloaks are for Aisling and Fachtna," said Manannán.

"Thanks, Man," said Fachtna, "they're the coolest gifts ever, aren't they Ais?"

"Deffo," she replied. "Thanks, Man."

"Manannán to you both," Dana corrected them. "My grandmother, Bláithín, must be wearing one of your invisibility cloaks," Aisling said cheekily to Manannán, her eyes glued to the banqueting room door which led down to the dungeons.

"Err—" He scowled, his face like a bulldog chewing a wasp.

"Where is she then? You said you set all the prisoners free when Dana asked."

"I said, 'more or less'," he retorted, his face flushed and fists clenched.

"You're a lying scumbag," Aisling was seething with rage. "Take me to my grandmother right now."

Dana, placing a calming hand on Aisling's shoulder, intervened. "I hadn't forgotten your grandmother, Aisling, but think about it, your grandad Aonghus is in for enough of a shock when you and Fachtna come home," she said quietly. "Blaithin's homecoming must not be overshadowed by yours. I propose we suggest to her that she stays with me for a day or two until I personally escort her home to Eamhain."

She turned to Manannán: "Bring us to Bláithín," she ordered, "and no more of your tricks." He hesitated momentarily, before leading them down a long corridor and stone stairs. The air was dank and foul-smelling. A shocked Aisling exclaimed: "How could you do this? You should be ashamed of yourself keeping an old lady hostage in this dirty hovel."

A poker-faced Manannán said nothing.

Fachtna whispered in her ear: "Bláithín's a tough cookie, just like you."

Aisling smiled. At the bottom of the stairs Manannán went into one of the cells and unlocked the chains that bound Bláithín. Aisling's heart pounded. It was scary to think that in a moment or two she would meet her grandmother for the first time.

"You can come in now," Manannán's voice called. "Bláithín is unfettered."

"Not until you come out," said Dana, nudging Aisling. "You go first," she urged. "I'll follow in a few moments."

"Do you want me to come with you?" Fachtna asked noting Aisling's sharp intake of breath.

"Yes, please." Aisling heaved a sigh of relief. "You can introduce me," she whispered.

But there was no need for introductions. Bláithín's flashbulb eyes lit up the dingy dungeon as she rushed over and hugged Aisling.

"I knew you'd come," she said. There was beauty and serenity in her aged face. "Your grandad is in for one big surprise." Her eyes twinkled with merriment. "You'll have to break the news to him. I wouldn't want to scare the pants off him," she said with a mischievous grin.

She clapped her hands and did a little dance for joy. Aisling and Fachtna cheered, which Dana took as her cue to come in. Aisling introduced Bláithín.

"Have you gathered all your belongings?" Dana asked.

"All except my book with the silver cover, in which I was recording the secrets of the *sídhe*," Bláithín answered, adding: "Oonagh confiscated it before Maebh and her *slua sídhe* brought me here."

"You'll get it back," Dana promised "I'll get our No-Name to fetch it later and bring it to my grove where hopefully you'll stay for a day or two while Aisling prepares Aonghus and Meg for your homecoming."

"Great! Aisling and I will work on it together during the summer holidays, won't we? It might make the bestseller list yet." Aisling, still a little overwhelmed, nodded her approval.

Dana led the way up the stone stairs and down the corridor to the banqueting room.

"I'll send you on a copy of the repossession order," she said to a dejected-looking Manannán as they trooped out. "And," she added, "no more of your double-dealing antics or you, Fand and your lovely daughters will find yourselves skating on thin ice."

Bláithín burst out laughing. "Picture them doing the splits on the Polar ice caps," she wise-cracked. Manannán just rolled his eyes heaven-wards. "Parting is such sweet sorrow," he said to Dana with a slasher smile. "Enbharr and my chariot are at your Majesty's disposal." He turned his back on them.

"Brill!" exclaimed Aisling rushing outside. She and Fachtna jumped on Enbharr's back and held on to its splendid mane.

Dana, Bláithín and No-Name sat into the gold chariot. Enbharr raced across the waters like the cold wind of spring, Manannán waved his cloak of mists behind them. When they got as far as the ninth wave Aisling saw what resembled a giant series of colourful curtains billowing across the sky and drew Fachtna's attention to them.

"It's mad," he said.

"Is it the Boring Alice thingmajig?" she asked.

Dana called out through the chariot window. "It's the Aurora Borealis. Particles of light blowing towards earth are colliding with gases in the atmosphere which make them glow and produce shades of blue, green, red and violet."

"Spooky!" said Aisling.

In the distance beyond the towering waves they could just about make out a coracle coming at speed towards them. Peals of laughter rippled through the waters. "It's the old sea-pirate himself in his Ocean Sweeper," Dana warned. "Brace yourselves." She threw her foxglove cape over Bláithín and shouted to Aisling to wrap hers around Fachtna. Manannán raised a furious wind whose howls and screams whipped Enbharr into a frenzy casting Aisling and Fachtna into the raging waters. Instantly, a mighty roar came from below the tumultuous waves. "It's Tonn Tuaige. They are safe," Dana said calmly to a terrified Bláithín. Lights twinkling like little stars appeared on the water as Aisling and Fachtna surfaced. They were smiling. Dana and Bláithín helped them into the chariot. "Tuag told us how Manannán, hearing of her dazzling beauty, sent his druid to Tara long ago to bring her to his sea palace, how his druid lulled her into a sleep, carried her body to the sea shore where he went in search of a coracle and how a great wave swept her out to sea," Aisling told them. "Manannán's blood-lust is not easily sated," said Dana.

Peals of laughter rippled a second time across the waves. Manannán, in coat of mail with gleaming breastplate, wearing

Ceannbarr, his helmet with two precious stones in front and one behind, brandishing the Freagarthach from whose wounds no mortal could recover, sat astride Draco, monster of the deep. Draco, breathing smoke and flames, opened its jaws and bared teeth sharper than searing knives. Steam flared from its nostrils as it bayed for blood. Three times Draco and his mount circled Enbharr and the golden chariot. The smoke and flames threatened to engulf it and burn all inside to a crisp, when a mighty roar came from beneath the waves, Tonn Rudhraighe erupted tsumani-like, and a giant wall of water struck with devastating force at breakneck speed, sucking Manannán and Draco into its swell, making them look like miniature super-surfers. Simultaneously, Dana's three-pronged spiral brooch emitted a high-pitched discordant tone that paralysed them both. Tonn Rudhraighe, froze momentarily before bulleting them outwards beyond Muruch's rock.

An uneasy silence followed. No-Name retreated behind Dana.

"Pity the Fear Dearg isn't with us," Aisling taunted him. "He could shrink you small enough to fit into a sliotar and Manannán wouldn't see you." No Name shrugged his shoulders.

Peals of laughter rippled across the waters a third time. Dana threw her eyes to heaven.

"Manannán, my old desperado, never gives up," she said.

"Come on, Manannán. Do your worst." Bláithín, shook her clenched fist at the thin air. Aisling and Fachtna laughed.

The wind changed. There was a phishing and a shrieking and a whistling from the heavens. Out of the mist a wake of buzzards, hawks and vultures appeared, soared into the air on the back of the wind, turned and plummeted downwards. A giant buzzard, its black eyes blazing fire and brimstone, landed on the front of the chariot and Kamikaze fashion, launched an attack with pointed talons. The mob of scrawny hawks and vultures, with increasing ferocity pecked holes in the roof until it cracked open. In one fell swoop they pounced on No-Name, tearing at his bushy beard and pecking at his eyes with their curved beaks.

Dana, composed as always, spoke this incantation.

Earth, Water, Fire, and Air
Keep us ever in your care.

A mighty thunderclap rent the sky, followed by the roar of the deep. Aisling and Fachtna shuddered as torrents of water surged into the chariot scattering the hawks and vultures. The giant buzzard took flight and as it soared upwards a cloak of many colours billowed in the wind. A bedraggled No-Name heaved a sigh of relief.

"Manannán, the old buzzard, will trouble us no more," Dana assured them. "He has bitten off more than he can chew. What you witnessed was the mighty Tonn Chliodhna. She, along with Tonn Tuaige and Tonn Rudhraighe, protects our waters as far as the ninth wave."

Enbharr neighed. Aisling and Fachtna climbed out of the chariot onto its back, held onto its splendid mane, and it raced across the waters and brought them to the trap door above the chunnel tunnel. It whinnied as Aisling and Fachtna dismounted. Dana tapped the waters with her ash wand and the trap door opened. They went down the seven stone steps and soon they heard a faint ratatata, ratatata, ratatata as the chunnel tram chugged to a halt.

Aisling and Fachtna sat in, chatting nineteen to the dozen.

"It won't be long until you are home," Dana said. "It's plain sailing from here on," she added with a glint in her eye.

The chunnel tram took off slowly at first, but then gathered speed. Dana took the controls, No Name sat beside Bláithín while Aisling and Fachtna ran upstairs chatting nineteen to the dozen. The tram slowed to a halt and Dana, Bláithín and No-Name got off. Aisling and Fachtna were nowhere to be seen. A perplexed No-Name searched high and low for them. Then giggling, they took off their invisibility cloaks, folded them and put them back into the silver acorns. If they fooled No-Name, they could fool anyone.

Three piebald stallions awaited them. Dana mounted one and No-Name hoisted himself up behind her. Fachtna helped Bláithín onto hers before he and Aisling took off. They raced through the dark tunnels, up the seven times seven steps back into the cave which led to the sea-shore and from there they galloped across across the land to Dana's grove. Before they went into the sacred chamber, Aisling and Fachtna helped themselves to some sloes and haws which grew outside.

Once inside her chamber Dana told Bláithín of her plans to establish an inter-world network where ideas could be exchanged for their mutual benefit. She suggested registering an official site,

www.ancientorderofthesidhe.ie

which they would administer together. In time, she said, they might even involve Manannán and the extra-terrestrials. They pledged to meet regularly to update the site which, she told Aisling, she and Bláithín would activate in double-quick sídhe time. Aisling and Fachtna were thrilled.

"No Name will see you both safely back to the wicker basket which will bring home," she said, "while Bláithín and I get down to business."

The stallions brought them to the wicker basket. Aisling scanned the floor and intentionally stepped on a red decorative knot in the shape of a sword and shield. As they waved goodbye she thought she detected a tear fall from No-Name's eye.

The basket started its journey up through the centre of the earth. At Dún Gréine, the trapdoor slid open and they blinked as they stepped into the sunlight. Aisling let out a huge sigh of relief and hugged Fachtna.

"Home at last," she said. They put on their invisibility cloaks and skipped along the road to Eamhain. They made their way through Bluebell Walk and O'Flaherty's cornfield, passed by the tall oak tree and the rowanberry bushes, walked down Foxglove Lane and crossed the garden fence into grandad Aonghus' cottage. They sat on the two-seater couch in front of the open fire. Aonghus was pouring his heart out to Meg: "I should have known she'd take off on her own, just like my—" He never finished the sentence because Aisling and Fachtna chose that very second to take off their invisibility cloaks. Aonghus and Meg were struck dumb. Jackie and Seán were sent for as well as Fachtna's grandad Senan, who was, as Aisling had suspected, Aonghus's boyhood friend.

Jackie, Aisling's mum, hugged her close and explained how a fortune teller had told her before Aisling's birth that her only daughter would take after her grandmother, Bláithín, a *sídhe* fanatic, who had mysteriously disappeared years before, which explained her mum's negative attitude to Seán's family and to the *sídhe*. Grandad, of course, was over the moon at the prospect of Bláithín's imminent home-coming which was the talk of Eamhain. The Eamhain Gazette dispatched teams of reporters and photographers to Dún Gréine where they set up camp between the sun fort and the hawthorn bush, awaiting Bláithín's return. The media got hold of the story. Grandad took the phone off the hook as there were so many calls from reporters all over the world hoping to get the first account of Aisling and Fachtna's adventures in the underworld and of course, Bláithín's imminent return. Seán, Aisling's dad, was looking at her with amusement.

"Is that weird looking emerald green cap you've on a fashion accessory in the underworld?" he asked. She raised her hand and as soon as she touched it, to everyone's astonishment, who do you think appeared in the centre of the kitchen floor but a smiling No-Name.

"And what," he asked, "is your next command?"

Aisling thought intently for a long time and then her eyes began to sparkle with some hidden excitement as she said...

But that, dear Reader, is another story entirely.

CORK CITY
LIBRARIES

Glossary

This story has many Irish names, words, and phrases in it, and it must be admitted that unless one has been lucky enough to study Irish, the spellings can look a little daunting. In the lists below a selection of words has been given, with a transcription in the International Phonetic Alphabet, and followed by a kind of "phrase-book" re-spelling in small capitals for readers unfamiliar with the IPA. (The IPA is not too difficult to learn, and the Wikipedia has several articles which may be useful to those who wish to learn more about Irish pronunciation.

http://en.wikipedia.org/wiki/Irish_phonology
http://en.wikipedia.org/wiki/Help:IPA_for_Irish
http://en.wikipedia.org/wiki/IPA

ar aghaidh libh! [er' 'ai l'iv'] (air EYE liv) away you go!

Ard-Rí ['a:rd 'ri:] (AHRD REE) High king

bean feasa [b'an 'f'asə] (BYAN FYASS-uh) a woman who forges links between *sídhe* and human.

bodhrán ['bo:ra:n] (BOH-rawn) a drum covered in goat-skin.

cearc [k'ark] (KYARK) hen

clóicín draíochta ['klo:k'i:n 'driəxtə] (KLOH-keen DREE-ukh-tuh) magic cloak

clurachán ['klurəxa:n] (KLOO-ruh-khawn) *pl.* **clurucháin** ['klurə-xa:in'] (KLOO-ruh-khoin) boozers and generally troublesome *sídhe*

coracle small rounded boat.

cos [kos] (KUSS) foot

deoch dearmaid [d'ox 'd'arəməd'] (DYOKH DYAR-uh-mid) a drink inducing forgetfulness

dúidín ['du:d'i:n'] (DOO-dyeen) *pl.* **dúidíní** ['du:d'i:n'i:] (DOO-dyee-nee) clay pipes

Fear Dearg [f'ar 'd'arəg] (FYAR DYAR-ug) otherworld being

féar gortach [f'e:r 'gortəx] (FYAIR GUR-tukh) 'hungry grass'. Anyone who stood on *féar gortach* suffered insatiable hunger pangs.

Freagarthach ['f'r'agərhəx] (FRAG-er-hukh) Manannán's sword, also called Retaliator. It never missed its mark.

geantraí ['g'antri:] (GYAN-tree) laughter provoking music; love song

geasa ['g'asə] (GYAS-uh) binding obligation

goltraí ['goltri:] (GUL-tree) lament

idir-ghabhálaí ['id'ir' ɣə'va:li:] (ID-yer ghu-VAW-lee) a go-between

lámh fhada [la:v 'adə] (LAWV AD-uh) a long arm

leipreachán ['l'ep'r'əxa:n] (LYEP-ra-khawn) *pl.* **leipreacháin** ['l'ep'r'əxa:in'] (LYEP-ra-khaw-in) a kind of *sídhe*, usually cobblers.

lios [l'is] (LISS) *pl.* **leasanna** ['l'asənə] (LYASS-uh-nuh) ring fort

muc [muk] (MOOK) pig

murúch ['muru:x] (MU-rookh) *pl.* **murúcha** ['muru:xə] (MU-roo-khuh) mermaids

Ogham ['o:əm] (OH-um) earliest form of writing found in Ireland.

ortha ['orhə] (UR-huh) charm, incantation

plamás ['plama:s] (PLAM-awss) flattery

púca ['pu:kə] (POO-kuh) horse/spirit

Samhain [sauin'] (SOW-in) Hallowe'en

sanctóir ['saŋkto:r'] (SANK-tor) sanctuary

saoi [suʲi:] (SEE) sage or wise person

skelp (from Irish *sceilp*) a slap, a thump

sídhe (*an older spelling for* sí) [ʃi:] (SHEE) invisible beings or spirits; hills, especially those associated with ancient archaeological sites. **bean sídhe** [b'a:n 'ʃi:] (BYAN SHEE) foreteller of death. **bobaireacht na sídhe** ['bobər'əxt nə 'ʃi:] (BOB-er-ukht nuh SHEE) trickery of the sídhe. **curracha sídhe** [kurəxə ʃiː] (KUR-uh-khuh SHEE) flat-bottomed boats. **leannán sídhe** [ˈlʲanaːn ʃiː] (LYAN-awn SHEE) invisible lover, muse as source of inspiration. **slua sídhe** [ˈsluə ʃiː] (SLOO-uh SHEE) a multitude of the sídhe

Sliocht sleacht ar shliocht bhur sleachta [ʃlʲixt ʃlʲaxt erʲ hlʲixt vur ʃlʲaxtə] (SHLIKHT SHLYAKHT air HLIKHT vur SHLYAKH-tuh) may your union be blessed with many future generations of children **sliotar** [ˈʃlʲitər] (SHLIT-er) *pl.* **sliotar** [ˈʃlʲitirʲ] (SHLIT-ir) a hurling ball. **Ó Sliotar Amú** (oh SHLIT-er a-MOO) a hurling ball astray

sparáin scillinge [ˈsparaːȷ̃n ˈʃkʲiliŋʲe] (SPA-roin SHKIL-ing-yuh) purses full of shilling coins

srón [sroːn] (SROHN) nose

suantraí [ˈsuəntriː] (SOO-uhn-tree) lullaby

tonn [taun] (TOWN) an ocean wave

torc [tork] (TORK) a gold neck ornament

tusa is mise [ˈtusəs ˈmʲiʃə] (TUSS-uh iss MISH-uh) you and me

uisce [ˈiʃkʲə] (ISH-kuh) water. **uisce beatha** [ˈiʃkʲə ˈbʲahə] (ISH-kuh BYA-huh) whiskey.

Personal names

Bébo [ˈbʲeːbo] (BAY-boh)

Bláithín Ní Mhurchú [ˈblaːhiːnʲ nʲiː ˈwurxuː] (BLAW-heen nee WUR-khoo)

Brigid [ˈbʲrʲiːdʲ] (BREED)

Cathbad [ˈkafad] (KAFF-ud)

Clíodhna [ˈkʲlʲiənə] (KLEE-uh-nuh)

Cogar and **Mogar** [ˈkogər, ˈmogər] (KUG-er, MUG-er)

Coinín [ˈkuȷ̃inʲiːnʲ] (KWIN-een)

Conán Maol Ó Dubhghaill [ˈkunaːn muᵻeːl oː ˈduːɣəlʲ] (KUN-awn MWAYL oh DOO-ghill)

Creidne [ˈkʲrʲedʲnʲə] (KRED-nyeh)

Cúchulainn [kuːˈxulɪnʲ] (koo-KHOOL-in)

Daghda [ˈdaɪdə] (DIGH-duh)

Darach [ˈdarəx] (DA-rukh)

Diarmuid and **Gráinne** [ˈdʲiərəmədʲ, ˈgraːnʲə] (DYIR-UH-mid, GRAW-nyuh)

Dr Cnámh Sídhe [knaːv ʃiː] (KNAWV SHEE)

Éadaoin [ˈeːdiːnʲ] (AY-deen)

Eisirt [ˈeʃɪrtʲ] (ESH-ert)

Fachtna Ó hAilpín [ˈfaxtnə oː ˈhalʲpʲiːnʲ] (FAKHT-nuh oh HAL-pin)

Feidhlim [ˈfʲailʲimʲ] (FYIGH-lim)

Fionán Mór Ó Dubhghaill [ˈfʲinaːn moːr oː ˈduːɣəlʲ] (FIN-awn MOAR oh DOO-ghill)

Fionnbharr [ˈfʲinvaːr] (FYIN-vahr)

Fir Bolg [fʲirʲ ˈbɔləg] (FEER BUL-ug)

Giob and **Geab** [gʲib, gʲab] (GIB, GYAB)

Glún [glu:n] (GLOON)
Grian ['g'r'iən] (GREE-uhn)
Goibniú ['guؚib'n'u:] (GWIB-nyoo)
Iubhdán ['u:da:n] (OO-dawn)
Labhraidh ['lauri:] (LOW-ree)
Luchtaine ['luxtən'ə] (LUKH-tuh-nyuh)
Lugh [lu:] (LOO)
Maebh[me:v] (MAYV)
Manannán ['manəna:n] (MAN-uh-nawn)
Neimhi ['n'ev'i] (NEV-ee)
Oghma ['o:mə] (OH-muh)
Oisín ['oʃi:n'] (USH-een)

Rudhraighe ['ruəri:] (ROO-uh-ree)
Seán Ó Cróinín [ʃa:n o: 'kro:n'i:n'] (SHAWN oh KROH-neen)
Sláinge ['sla:ŋ'ə] (SLAW-ngyeh)
Srón and Sleamhain [sro:n, 'ʃl'auən'] (SROAN, SHLYAW-in)
Tuag, Tonn Tuaige [tuəg, taʊn 'tuəg'ə] (TOO-ug, TOWN TOO-ig-yuh)
Tuatha Dé Danann ['tuəhə d'e: 'danən] (TOO-uh-huh DYAY DAN-un)

Place-names

Brugh na Bóinne [bru: nə 'boɪn'ə] (BROO nuh BOY-nyeh)
Cruachan ['kruəxən] (KROO-uh-khun)
Doire an Chairn ['dirən 'xar'in'] (DER-uh un KHAR-in)
Dún Gréine [du:n 'g'r'e:n'ə] (DOON GRAY-nyuh)

Eamhain ['avən'] (AV-win)
Lupra and Luprachán ['luprə, 'luprəxa:nؚ] (LOOP-ruh, LOOP-ruh-khawn)
Sliabh Bheatha ['ʃl'iəv v'ahə] (SHLYEE-uv VA-huh)
Tír na nÓg ['t'i:r' nə no:g] (TYEER nuh NOAG)